GENERATION Curse?

Colleen Smith-Dennis

LMH PUBLISHING LIMITED

© 2016 Colleen Smith-Dennis
First Edition
10 9 8 7 6 5 4 3 2 1

Editor: K. Sean Harris
Cover Illustration: Courtney Lloyd Robinson
Cover Design: Sanya Dockery
Book Design, Layout & Typesetting: Sanya Dockery

Published by LMH Publishing Limited
Suite 10-11, Sagicor Industrial Park
7 Norman Road
Kingston C.S.O., Jamaica
Tel.: (876) 938-0005;
Fax: (876) 759-8752
Email: lmhbookpublishing@cwjamaica.com
Website: www.lmhpublishing.com and www.lmhdigital.com

Printed in the U.S.A.   ISBN: 978-976-8245-40-3

NATIONAL LIBRARY OF JAMAICA CATALOGUING-IN-PUBLICATION DATA

Smith-Dennis, Colleen
    Generation curse? / Colleen Smith-Dennis

    pages; cm.

ISBN 978-976-8245-40-3 (pbk)

1. Jamaican fiction   I. Title

813   dc 23

CONTENT

Rita

It was only 5 p.m. but already most of the night people who frequented the shops in the village square were present. They sat on the floor of the shop piazza, some leaning against the wall. Others sat on stools taken from inside the shop, while a few leaned across the shop counter hiding the glass case displaying cosmetics, hair products and school items.

The shopkeeper, Mr. Lazarus, was unhurriedly parcelling flour. There were white smudges on his shallow forehead and on his long cheeks. His face was emaciated with bones protruding from his jaws. His eyes were huge and sunken. His whole face reminded one of death, he might have been to the grave and came back after the maggots had eaten away his flesh. He was not a loud or frequent talker, and the latter was strange since most of the village gossip took place in and around his shop. His brain was an archive of village occurrences. If he were really persuaded he

1

could recount events from sixty years before and challenge any-one who misrepresented details or omitted them. Behind his back people called him Member Head. His wife, Miss Laza, was sitting in the doorway to the back storage room, checking the list of creditors and how much they owed.

The anger of the summer sun was fading and the azure sky was almost cloudless, save for a few straggling white clouds that were drifting over to the few bright coloured ones that lightly glowered in the west. A kite of swallow going home dotted the sky.

"Mr. Laza pour out a round a whites fi everybody in here," Mr. Amos ordered, taking out his wallet to look for the money. He had just got his coffee bonus and was returning a kindness he himself had often benefitted from when he had no money. His brown, laughing eyes lit up with the pride of a father holding his first newborn son.

Mr. Laza wiped his hands on a towel on the counter, silently counting the number of men in the shop and then took out the glasses from a small glass section over the liquor side of the shop. Under the hawk-like watch of the men, he poured the liquor into the glasses and then placed a jug of water on the table for them to add whatever they wanted to.

As they were drinking, Big Head and Philton came inside and greeted them, and lifted the domino table that was behind the shop door. The table was placed on the piazza and some of those sitting on the stools moved them around the table. Philton did not sit with them. He went around the back and started setting up the music boxes.

At that moment Mr. Herald walked in, bearing heavily on his cane. Despite his halting walk he would not stay away from the night life. His nickname was Green Lizard. The story had been told that one day Mr. Herald went to the bushes with a group of work men. They were there to chop bush and clear the ground for a yam garden. As was the custom, the women would either cook and take the food for the men, or the men would cook their own food in a kerosene tin or old, black Dutch pots. Mr. Herald was the chief cook and he really outdid himself with the huge cartwheel dumplings and massive chunks of yellow yam. He cooked some salt mackerel in a cheese tin and made some lemonade in another kerosene tin.

He left the food to finish cook and then went back to work. At lunch time the hungry hoard of men sat on the grass, ready for their meal. Mr. Herald got the bruised tin plates and opened the tin with the yam and dumplings only to see a well-cooked green lizard posing at the top of the pot. Everyone refused to eat the food, that is, everyone except Mr. Herald. He would not see his effort wasted so he ate the sumptuous meal and became known forever as Green Lizard.

It was he who came with the latest gossip. No sooner had he seated himself on a stool and ordered a drink than he blurted out, "Guess what mi just hear?"

Everyone stopped what he or she was doing and turned to Mr. Herald.

"What happen now Greeny?" Mr. Amos asked, anxious to partake in discussing the latest gossip.

Mr. Herald, glad to be the focus of attention, sipped his drink before answering, thereby building up suspense. While everyone waited, he wiped his moustache with the back of his hand and settled himself comfortably on the stool.

"Lawd Greeny what you a hold on to so long? You always announce things and then take forever to talk bout them." Mr. Amos pouted and hissed his teeth, turning his back to Mr. Herald.

Finally he said, "You know Miss Harmond daughter, Rita, that married to Pete up the hill?"

"Greeny what you mean if we know Rita? Nuh here so all of us come from. How you mean if we know her?" Big Head stared at him incredulously, hissed his teeth and took up the dominoes.

"Guess what, the baby she was expecting nuh born dead again!" Mr. Herald announced.

"What! Again!" several voices chorused. Everyone on the outside had crowded into the shop by now and began to give their opinion.

"But this is the fourth baby that born dead, plus what she lose otherwise!" one man announced.

"No sah is five of them now," said Mr. Laza forcefully. "Almost one every year fi the last six years."

"But Jesus mercy dem people really curse as people in the village think!" one man shouted as if the people he was talking to were deaf or far away.

"Four pickney dead in four years! Why she nuh stop kill off herself?" another commented.

"Dat deh family really curse fi true. Five dead, not even one alive! Instead of counting pickney, she a count grave!" Mr. Amos added. "An' the worse part of it is that Mr. Clement treat her so bad! Him know say she come out a no good family so him nuh really care for she."

"Nothing good don't ever come out a that family," Mr. Bates put forward.

"From her grandfather time till now that family just like a scourge on the face a the earth. Everything just go bad for them, from her grandfather time till now," Mr. Lazarus observed in one of his rare comments.

"You member one time when all a dem over Gully Deep look like dem did want to kill off dem one another? Parents an' pickney a fight, pickney an' pickney a fight," Miss Laza, encouraged by her husband's contribution, recalled.

One by one they all recalled the family's ill fortune and commented on the curse which seemed to have afflicted the family over the years. Everywhere they went the curse seemed to follow them; from country to town and back again. What had this family done that was causing this problem?

E E E

Mrs. Harmond walked from her backyard and sat on a stone at the side of the house. It was late afternoon, the birds were calling to one another as they made their way home. Their calls were raucous and shrill as though they were quarrelling about something: spoils not equally shared, invasion of their nests or unfaithful mates. For a while Mrs. Harmond just sat and drifted into their lives, imagining this and that and though she imagined that they too had problems, she envied them the privilege of flying away from it and never returning. Flying away and leaving it all to another member of the family or a kind, concerned neighbour. As she listened, the popular song surfaced in her mind, *If I had a wing like a dove, if I had a wing like a dove, I would fly, fly away, fly away and be at rest.*

While she listened to the birds' dispute, she heard another sound, a small whimpering which was different from the discordant cries. She turned her head to the sound and smiled knowingly. She would have known without looking; it was the hawks. They had swooped down on a family of petcharies nesting in a nearby mango tree who were putting up a defence. She did not like the hawks, too many of her baby chickens had been abducted by these rapacious accipitridae. She got up and searched the ground for a small stone and threw it at the offending birds closest to her. It didn't hit them but went close enough to send them flying away. But they were not the only ones that flew off; the birds that were being molested, not knowing who the missile was intended for, flew away too. They squawked and chirped fiercely, continuing the bickering in flight.

A call from near the bottom of the gully forced her attention from the birds.

"Miss Harry! Miss Harry oh!" The voice sounded anxious and urgent. "Miss Harry, Miss Harry oh where are you?"

"Roun' di houseside, ah sitting roun' di houseside," she answered, not getting up. She recognized the voice and knew that Brother Gustus could find her anywhere on her property if he wanted to. She also knew that he had come to bring her bad news. He was her nearest neighbour and often came by, but mostly to bring her the latest gossip from the village when it pertained to her and to lament her misfortune. He was eighty-five years of age, but that did not prevent him from being everywhere there was something to talk about. He came around the corner of the house, using his stick to assist him in his slow walk towards her. His bleary, cat eyes were bright with unmasked excitement and an emotion undefined. Even though the dusk was slowly creeping in to consume the land, she could see the front of his shiny, bald head. His white hair only grew from the middle to the back of his head and every time he went to the barber he quarrelled with him for charging him full price when he only had half a head of hair. His ears, which were disproportionate to his face in terms of their largeness, always stood straight and alert like antennas ready to absorb every bit of gossip and disperse it to all and sundry, even though he maintained that he never discussed people's business.

He came towards her and leaned on his stick, eyeing her critically. "But Harry a so you just sit down easy like when cat jus' eat an' him belly full. I t'ink you would be up by Rita now giving her support. Ah don't understand you!" His voice was filled with incredulity.

"What you mean up by Rita giving her support?" Mrs. Harmond was taken aback by the comment.

"You never know that she due an' that she have the baby an' it dead as usual!" Mr. Gustus informed her loudly.

"How you mean have the baby an' it dead after nobody don't come and call me. She not suppose to have it till the nex' two week! That's what she tell me when me see her yesterday." She emphasized the last three words as she got down off the stone.

Mr. Gustus was ready with some criticism but the look on her flesh toned face, spattered with black moles of various sizes silenced him. Her black, sour sop seed eyes dimmed considerably as she looked away from him and started singing, *What a friend we have in Jesus* in a sorrowful, slow manner, slurring every word. He looked with interest at the long, thin, gaulin neck and marvelled anew at its ability to hold her angular face and head in place. She straightened the grey and black head tie that she was wearing with hands that bore gnarled, prominent red veins that threatened to burst through the mottled skin. Her palms were home to calluses which flourished as a result of the machete she often wielded when tending to her garden. The outer part of her fingers were decorated with scratches and cuts of various lengths and shapes which would make hardened soldiers glad to accept her as one of them.

She walked into the house without looking back at Mr. Gustus. He watched the small figure with her musical 'step up and down the scale' gait which had characterized her movement ever since he had known her as a much younger woman. It had become only slower and more pronounced, and since she was always singing, especially in times of trouble, it seemed natural for her steps to sing along with her.

"Jerome! Jerome!" she called loudly as she reached the long verandah which spanned the length of the two-bedroom house. "Jerome come here now." Not waiting for him to answer or come she continued, "Ah going up by Rita now an' since nobody else not here right now, don't bodder to leave the house. You hear me bwoy?"

"Yes Mama," answered an irritable voice from inside one of the two bedrooms.

"Make certain now. An' if ah don't come back by time night come down one a you bwoy come meet me."

Not waiting for an answer she picked up her stick and went back outside. Her feet moved in unison with her musical gait. Mr. Gustus tried to keep up with her but was finding it difficult.

"Harry since the t'ing happen a little time now an' nobody never call you why you trying to bruk your neck now?"

"Well you know jus' like anybody else that this is not her first misfortune," Mrs. Harmond stated.

"Not her first time! Everybody know dat she have one dead pickney every year!" Mr. Gustus pointed out in case Mrs. Harmond had forgotten.

"Well since is my daughter ah know that so you don't need to shout at me." She pouted and quickened her steps, hoping he would take the hint and go back to his home.

Even though it was painful, Mr. Gustus started to walk faster. "Well she didn't call you an' you is her mother. Why you think she do that?" His tone willed her to answer the question.

"How should I know that? Maybe she have a good reason. I will find that out myself." Her voice suggested that she had ended the conversation but he persisted.

"Well because of the curse she maybe t'ink you tired to come see dead pickney." His voice was low and blunt.

"What curse? I never know that you join with careless people to call down bad luck on my family!" Mrs. Harmond was angry. She was almost out of the gully and was now climbing up the hill. She turned around and gave him an evil look. His comment had only exacerbated the situation. "I can't stop you or anybody else from going up to Rita, but don't follow me. Let me go an' deal wit' my curse myself!" With that she stomped off and left him.

When she got to her daughter's house there were only a few people there. She thought to herself that since the baby was not someone that anybody knew or was accustomed to, that was expected. There were about five people on the veranda but Rita was not one of them. She greeted them as warmly as she could and they did the same without really looking directly at her.

Rita was sitting up by herself at the opened back door of the small living room. She looked around when she heard the thumping of her mother's stick. Mrs. Harmond noticed her last child's huge eyes, which had become perpetually sad. Her face seemed to have lengthened even more than it had before and the black eyes stared emptily out of their sockets and refused to focus on any-thing in particular. Her long, unprocessed hair looked limp and lacked lustre. Even though it was customary for women to gain weight during pregnancy, she was as thin and flat as an iron

9

board, no one would have ever known she had ever been pregnant if he or she had not been told. The sleeveless dress she wore hung like an oversized, misfitted gown on her bony body. Her arms were long and gangling as if they belonged to a taller person.

Mrs. Harmond's eyes filled with tears as she looked at Rita. The pain she felt defied description. She hobbled over to her daughter's side and sat beside her for more than fifteen minutes before she could utter a word. She simply did not know what to say, did not know what explanation to offer or how to inspire hope. Her thoughts were a maelstrom of unconnected symbols swirling around in clockwise and anti-clockwise directions. She hugged her. Rita's body heaved and shook in her arms but she did not speak, only a barely discernable whimper escaped from her. She grasped her like a member of the Simian group climbing a tree. Mrs. Harmond rocked her to and fro praying silently, not really knowing what she was asking.

She did not leave as early as she thought she would because the few people who were there earlier had left and Rita's husband had not come home. Three of her grandchildren came to meet her and to cheer their aunt but she took no notice of them. She had been transported to another world where she did not have to feel or think and oblivion was bliss.

When Pete came, he greeted them coldly, and then went into the second bedroom without exchanging another word with anyone. He did not look at his wife and when Mrs. Harmond went to the room door, knocked and told him that she wanted to talk to him, he did not respond.

"You need to take Rita to hospital Pete because she not doing so well. Member that the doctor did say she should come in one week before she have the baby, but the baby come before time an' she really not well now. Ah think she need to see a doctor, some-thing not right at all."

There was still no answer from the bitter, childless man. He did not even make one sound. It was as though they had imagined someone going inside. Mrs. Harmond made a quick decision. "Jen," she turned to her granddaughter who had come to meet her, "stay with Rita tonight, ah just don't feel to leave her by her-self, something more than physical wrong with her. Ah going down a yard to see to things an' ah will come up early in the morning to take her to doctor myself cause it too late now for me to get anything to carry her. When we gone you can go to the post office an' go talk to the post office lady bout the death." She sounded tired and defeated.

"But Mama, me hear that the baby done bury aready," Jen protested.

"Yes, but you still have to make it official."

"So what bout Mr. Pete, why him don't go cause I don't know the details." Jen was looking for a way out of the distasteful job.

"I not even going to ask him anything cause it look like him really don't want anything to do wit' us." Her voice had a slight tremor but she held her head up and kissed her daughter, promising to return early the next morning to take her to the doctor. Rita held on to her mother like a drowning woman seeking rescue. Mrs. Harmond held her and then took her into the unoccupied bedroom to lie down. She told Jen not to leave her side.

Mrs. Harmond stepped out into the dark night. The moon was on leave and only a few lonely stars tried to make up for its absence. They failed miserably and Mrs. Harmond had to rely on the flashlight that Melvin had bought. She took a shortcut through the bushes because she did not want to walk on the main road and encounter the disingenuous community people who wanted to pry, give advice and look at her like a discarded dirty rag. Jerome and Melvin, sensing their grandmother's mood, kept quiet and slowed their pace considerably so that she did not have to hurry too much. Mrs. Harmond was immersed in the events of the past which were chiefly as dark as the night itself.

There were some things that she held at bay in her subconscious which would only derail her mental stability if she allowed them to surface. They were often derided in the community because many people thought her family was cursed. As she remembered it the notion came about because it was said her father had stolen Parson Keith's bull and then burnt the manse. History also had it that he had wanted to kill Parson Keith. Despite the many criminal acts which took place in the community, most people at that time professed godliness and in their own way revered the church, which for them meant the building and the leaders. This did not prevent them from heaping criticisms on the clergy when they deemed it necessary. Her father had fled the district since and had never been seen again. They had to live with the shame and dis-grace and what was known as the family curse for many years. Her own husband had left for England leaving the six children in her care. Like her father, he had never been seen or heard from again. She had raised the six children with ages ranging from fourteen to three with very little help from the husband's family.

The children had not done well and sometimes got into trouble but nonetheless three of them made it to Great Britain. It was both positive and negative; positive because they were able to put the community and their poverty behind them and launch out afresh, and negative because they had left ten of the children in her care with only an occasional visit, a few pounds monthly and a yearly parcel of mostly already worn 'ole bruk' clothes for her to raise them on. She sympathized with them because she knew their poor financial standing but even though she was hesitant to admit it, she felt she had done her share of child rearing and needed a break so that she could go to her grave in peace, in one piece.

The children were hard to manage and despite her mantra, 'good behaviour, honesty and education will take you a far way', she had a difficult time. They knew no other parent, but she told them that love was more concrete in action than words. Two sets of parents were married and the other one was single. They had promised to file for them but to date not one had reached the promised land and their ages and behaviour would soon render this hopeless.

If it weren't for them she could have stayed with Rita but she had to secure the few pounds she had just received before it disappeared into nothingness and everybody in the house would swear innocence and malice her for suspecting them.

When she got in, it was 11p.m. but still the four older boys were not home as yet. She was too tired to question and quarrel so she went to her bed. Two of the girls shared the bed with her and the other one slept in the hall on a three-quarter bed. She slept fitfully that night and her two dogs, Rusty and Nip, competed to see who could bark the loudest and longest that night. They howled like their descendant, the wolf, and sent frightening shivers down her back that travelled to her toes. She shoved aside the belief that the howling sounds were signalling death and wondered if other dogs had come down to the house or if strangers were around. In addition she could swear that at one time she heard the cry of an abner. She wondered if the dead baby had followed her home. She got up and read two Psalms and commanded it to go back to its resting place where it would be better off than this old, evil world.

She got up at 6:00 a.m. with a raging headache. She knew that it was a tension headache brought on by her daughter's situation so she decided not to take any tablets but leave it to calm down in time. As soon as she had a bath, she tied a cloth soaked in alcohol around her forehead. She had promised to go by Rita early and she felt something propelling her to move fast.

Everyone was fast asleep when she went outside with her old, black handbag packed for emergency. As she stepped outside the sound of the birds welcomed her. The black birds were loudest. There were also three silent crows circling close to the pasture. She wondered if the dogs had killed another animal last night and the wind had passed on the message so early to them. She heard the baby chicken cry and was just in time to see the hawk making off with it. It was the last baby chicken for the brown hen. She ran out of the bushes and started squawking. If she had not gone up to Rita, she would have put it in the coop with the other chickens last night.

As she stood there lamenting hers and the hen's loss, she saw a figure running down the hill at olympic speed. Her heart did a fast cartwheel and the pain in her head banged at her forehead. Her feet dissolved beneath her as she started walking towards the runner.

When he was a few metres away she recognized 'Who Dat', whose given name was Lenville Murray. Everyone called him Who Dat because the story was told that one day Mr. Noels, who owned one of the biggest properties in the community, was walking in his vast yam garden. As he walked he detected a slight movement and heard a faint rustling sound. Frightened, he shouted out, "A who dat?"

A voice answered back, "A who dat?"

Mr. Noels was certainly not blessed with tolerance especially for thieves so he shouted out again, "A who dat?" Infuriated, he advanced on the person shouting, "A who dat a ask a who dat when me a ask a who dat?"

Lenville ran out of the garden leaving the bag of yam he had filled to steal. Mr. Noels added more and more to the story each time he told it. Soon the whole community had heard and everyone started calling Lenville, Who Dat.

When he reached Mrs. Harmond, he could hardly breathe or stand.

"Miss Harry," he gasped, huffing and puffing like a steam engine which had climbed a steep hill. "You need to come right now cause Miss Rita not moving and her eyes them close."

He had run out of gas completely and he sat down on the ground, his chest heaving as if it was going to burst.

Mrs. Harmond did not say anything. She walked even faster though she could not feel her feet beneath her. Who Dat caught up with her a few minutes later after his heart had quieted down.

When they got to the house there was a huge crowd. Mrs. Harmond's son, Markdon, hurried towards her.

"Mama ah don't believe it." Tears snaked down his face.

"What you don't believe?" asked his mother.

Markdon looked at her as though she had lost her mind. "Mama ah don't believe that Rita dead." He said the words slowly so that they could penetrate the mental blockade he thought she had erected.

"Dead! Who dead?" She looked from him to the house and then she hit Who Dat with her walking stick.

"But Miss Harry is not me kill har, what you licking me for?" He backed away from her, disbelief jumping into his eyes.

"You didn't tell me she dead!" she screamed at him.

"Ah tell you dat she not moving an' dat her eyes close, an' if dat is not dead then ah don't know what else is! The people say ah should tek time an' tell you an' ah did." He backed away in the crowd looking offended and wondering if Mrs. Harmond was alright. For a moment everything grew dim and took on a hazy appearance; they danced near and far in front of her in a ghostly blur. She closed her eyes and found relief in the darkness. A few seconds later she opened her eyes and the trees and figures around her moved in glazed haziness and then settled down and took on distinct shapes.

"Mama! Mama! Jesus have mercy you okay! You okay? Mama answer mi nuh, you okay?" Markdon's anxious voice boomed in her ears.

"Yes son, ah fine, ah fine, don't worry yuhself ah going to be okay." She straightened up and then forced herself to focus. All around her there were concerned voices and looks.

"Miss Harry you okay?"

"Miss Harry you have to keep up."

"Miss Harry don't bother drop down on us!"

Jen pushed herself through the crowd and came to her. "Mama, Mama, oh lawd Mama!" She hugged her grandmother and then led her inside and through the back door. Markdon accompanied them. Mrs. Harmond did not look inside the room where Rita's body lay.

When they got outside, one of her other sons, Tobias, was waiting for her. He hugged her and then led her to an old bench close to the butchery. Some of her grandchildren came out of the house and stood around her.

"Jen what happen, what really happen? Ah know that Rita was really sick but ah never expect her to jus' get up an' dead so." Her voice trembled like a bowl of jelly.

"Mama it strange, really strange for true. Ah was lying down beside her an' ah tried to talk to her. But she only grunt an' one time she say 'Dem come for me, all four a dem come for me'. When I ask her who, she didn't answer. She get up one time an' go into the hall. Then she go drink water, come back an' fall asleep an' then I fall asleep to. Then early down into the three o' clock hours she start making some strange sound like she a choke an' struggle with someone, an' me run an' call Maas Pete. Him tek a little time to come an' when him come him ask me why me nuh give her some water. Me tell him say she never ask me fi any. Him go outside an' then him come back with a cup of water an' him give her to drink. After she drink it, it look like she drop asleep. Me could hardly sleep again cause the dog dem a carry on an' a howl an' some whole heap a something a cry-cry all round the house. When day start peep out now me a check to see if she okay an' only to fine say she stiff out an' all me a call her she don't move nor answer, but her face look like she a laugh, you know the little funny way she always look when she get a joke. Then me run an' bawl out fi Maas Pete an' him come an' start shout say she dead." Jen was sobbing uncontrollably. "Imagine she dead an' me lie down beside her de whole time, suppose her duppy did choke me!"

"Jen ah know how you feel but stop chat rubbish. Rita wouldn't harm a fly in this world." Mrs. Harmond defended her dead daughter.

The autopsy revealed that Rita had died of an overdose of pills. The doctor surmised that she was already weak after her delivery that day and so her body did not really have the strength to fight. Mrs. Harmond was present when the autopsy was being done. Her two sons who had accompanied her opted to stay outside. Mrs. Harmond knew the fresh spate of gossip that would result from the news that Rita had killed herself. She also knew that the church would not want to give her a Christian funeral, so she called the pathologist aside and had a frenzied, whispered conversation with him. When she got the death certificate it read reason for death, heart attack, and that was what everyone including Rita's husband, all the members of the family and the community were told. Her husband, who had worn a strange look on his face since the death looked relieved; a natural cause was better than a spiritual one.

The community at large had performed their own autopsy and had declared that her dead children had taken her to look after them. Mrs. Harmond told some of them that she had never heard such 'chupidness' in her entire life. It had also become an exposed secret that Pete was trying to disguise his happiness of the freedom he now had to find another woman and beget even one child. Some people were glad at the prospect while others criticised him for they claimed he had not been kind to her and there were whispers of spousal abuse that Mrs. Harmond had not heard of before. The community was also rocked with stories of ghostly sightings. Those living close by and those who had gone to 'set up' each night with Pete claimed they had seen Rita with her four children behind her. One person said on one occasion she had the last baby in her hand and the other bigger ones standing around her. Mrs. Harmond asked Mr. Herald who told her the news a few days after the death if dead people could grow. Since the babies had all died at birth how could they all be bigger and standing? She told him she had no time for idle people who never liked the family before and were taking every opportunity to hurt them even more.

The night before the funeral when they were at the wake the rumour spread that Miss Nate had locked herself and her family in her house because as it turned dusk, five weird-looking black birds had taken up residence beside the tank in front of her house and were making strange sounds so she was afraid to come out. Rita had often gone to her house to get water so of course it was she and her children. Mrs. Harmond hissed her teeth and continued to serve the bread and sprat.

After the funeral everyone marvelled at Mrs. Harmond's fortitude. She did not shed a single tear; like the Rock of Gibraltar, she bore it all, at least outwardly. She graciously accepted the sympathy whether it was genuine or not, she shook proffered hands, withstood hugs and kept a straight face. Some thought that when she saw the four nameless mounds marked only by wooden crosses beside her daughter's fresh grave she would have rained tears. Mrs. Harmond's resilience had come through, her resolve not to break down before the crowd stood fast.

She would do her mourning in her own way, in her own time, as she digested and ruminated on certain information.

The Coming of Nickar's Father

Nickar sat at the top of the hill and looked down into Gully Deep, his home for seventeen years. Much of the district was hilly but a few people owned land which plunged many feet below the level of the hills. It was a natural formation and not mined out and left by a bauxite company as many would suppose. There were a number of copses and grassy areas interspersed by shrubs and rare green plants. Gardens with yam, peas, potatoes, corn, cassava, peanut and other crops were sometimes grown in the area by family members or Mrs. Harmond's grandsons, when they felt moved to do so. They were not motivated to farm as they saw it as a hard non-income earner which should be done by elderly people. At times they did not have a problem with reaping what other people sowed, though they vehemently denied it, even if they were caught in the act.

Nickar had not gone to school past grade nine. The discipline of getting up early, walking two miles to the new secondary school, sitting quietly in classes and pretending to learn when he was hungry, was certainly not one of his favourite past times. He wanted to have nothing to do with books except to move them out of his way if they got in it. And he was not the only one, he reasoned, four of the nine cousins who lived at Gully Deep all seemed to share the same sentiment that school was not for them and their grandmother could not force them to go even though she had threatened to report them to the police. Her admonition that schooling could help to reduce their poverty was not heeded. It was their belief that schooling was for people who came from good families or who already had money and were smart. He and his brother had none of these privileges. What they had was a curse hanging over their heads and what could anyone do to remove a curse? You just had to go along with it. Look at what had happened to his Aunt Rita who was as gentle and harmless as a newborn. He grimaced as he thought of his aunt and his mud-coloured face took on a serious, frightening look which spread to his intense black eyes. He had not cut his hair for a few months despite his grandmother's anger and pleas. This only added to his feral look. His hair struck out from his head as if it were in malice. It was not as if he had embraced the Rastafarian faith, it was a sign of defiance and rebellion.

His brother Tyrone, who was two years younger, had decided to follow the same path of dropping out of school. He however, had an uncanny sense of neatness. His hair had to be properly trimmed, an activity he performed himself, and his clothes were also neat and well co-ordinated. He was Mr. Dapper himself, a trait he was told he had inherited from a father he never knew; a father he was told was a slick thief who had fathered many children and left them to survive on the mercy of fate. The community commentary stated that there was no way the boys could come to anything good. They were cursed on every side. Their one sister, Joan-Ann, probably had a better chance as her father was a different man who had mistakenly got himself mixed up in the Harmond family. He came from a family of people with good reputation that the parson's father had known for a long time. Maybe if she had been raised in the father's family then she would have turned out differently than what she was now, a fourteen-year-old teenage girl who was very often at one of the shops' piazza with the other girls whose parents seemed to have lost control of them. The few people in the community who really knew the truth knew that her father had migrated to England and was living with Joan-Ann's mother. They had promised to file for her but hardly sent anything to the grandmother for her maintenance, let alone to file. She told everyone she was going to England and when she went to school she refused to go to classes. Her grandmother warned her that a dunce and a black one at that would not get very far in a foreign country where you were only a third-class citizen and that was if she ever got there. Joan-Ann did not listen, her head was in the sky and she was only interested in two things, going to England and boys.

Nickar had plans in his head and he was going to carry them out. The first one at the moment was to get something to eat after he came in off the road that night. Dinner was always early and everyone got hungry right after, for the last few nights no one had gone out to the village square because of the stories that were being circulated about Rita's ghost. He had to get the food and prepare it before nightfall so that he did not have to stay alone in the outdoor kitchen when everyone was telling stories.

He got up and made his way towards Mr. Heron's farm. Mr. Heron's name could not have been more apt. Some of the children called him 'Bird'. He was tall and thin with legs that could only be found on a mannequin. Their movements were robot-like. His small lizard-face had a bill for a nose. He owned an extensive property which adjoined their neighbour, Mr. Gustus' land. There were a large number of coconut trees and an even larger orange grove. In addition to those fruits there were mango, jackfruit, sweet sop, sour sop, naseberry, apples, starapple and breadfruit trees. There seemed to be everything on the land including ground provision. Many people in the village made a living planting and reaping, and also stealing and then selling from this farm. Lately, Mr. Heron had erected rolls and rolls of barbed wire around his property because he was losing almost as much as he reaped. He also vowed to chop to bits and feed to his many dogs anyone who was caught on his property without permission.

Nickar had sought employment on the farm a few times but he did not like the long hours, the hard work and the small pay, being a proletariat did not appeal to him. He knew the property well and he knew how to get on and off without having to crawl through the barbed wire. He made his way as stealthily as a cat stalking a lizard. He parted the profuse shrubbery with much ease and the full length jeans pants he had put on for this purpose protected his legs from the cow-itch which clawed cruelly at him. He gathered some bush and grass and made a high raised bed so that when he threw down the breadfruit, they would not be battered.

There was a small ackee tree growing just outside the barbed wire fence. It was not really on Mr. Heron's property but one could climb into it and then transfer to the breadfruit tree with the big yellow heart breadfruit, much better for eating than the small white heart ones at the back of his house. He rolled his pants and shinnied up the ackee tree as if it were his habitat. The fruit looked even better at close range than they did from the ground and he almost licked his lips in anticipation of the feast he would have with hot roasted breadfruit with butter and roasted saltfish.

He had decided to pick six and was wringing off the last one when the accident happened. He had not seen the duck ants nest close to the breadfruit he was picking. As he started wringing the breadfruit, he felt them crawling over his hand. He knew what they were and decided not to panic but when they started biting him and the message hit his brain, it was too painful to bear. His hand fell from the breadfruit and he lost his footing and started falling. He felt himself diving feet first into nothingness and then he stopped. He emitted a scream that could be heard for miles away. His clothes were caught in the barbed wire which was tearing mercilessly into his skin. He tried to extricate himself but only became more entangled. He screamed louder as the pain became more excruciating. He lost consciousness and then he came back to his senses and started screaming again.

It was Mr. Gustus who heard the screams. "Miriam," he said to his wife who was pulling in the last goat to tie it up close to the house. "Miriam you hear anything?"

"Yes, it sound like some careless pickney dem down a Sister Harry a carry on with them foolishness." She hissed her teeth and pulled the protesting goat behind her.

The sound came again, mournful and piteous. The dogs started barking and rushed towards the sound, and so did Mrs. Gustus as she called to her small grandson.

"Earle! Earle you better go down the gully and call for help cause somebody close by in trouble!"

25

"No," said Mr. Gustus, "him can move faster than you, let him look is what an' you go down a Gully for help!"

Always obedient, she complied and while he went towards the sound, she rushed down the hill shouting, "Sister Harry, Jen, Melvin help oh! Nickar, Tyrone help oh help somebody up so in trouble!" She was breathless, walking fast was not a part of her routine anymore. Pain was slanting down her knees but she kept on calling.

Simone, Jen, Tyrone and Mrs. Harmond ran out as she came into the yard proper.

"All a you deaf inside there, somebody a bawl fi help up the hill!"

Everyone dashed off leaving Mrs. Harmond and Mrs. Gustus to catch up. When they were half way up Earle rushed down to them, falling into the grass when he almost reached them.

He picked himself up and shouted out, "Is Nickar, him drap in a baab wire an' him can't get out. Him a bleed bad bad!" He ran back up the hill without waiting for a response.

Mrs. Harmond began to sing "Oh what a friend, what a precious friend" in an off-key, melancholy voice.

Mrs. Gustus looked at her and did not know what to say. She looked at the sky at a group of screaming blackbirds and noticed the crows circling overhead, diving downwards then upwards and circling again.

When they reached the area, except for the talking from the small crowd which had gathered, Nickar was quiet. His brother and another man were holding him up while someone was using a saw to cut the barbed wire. While this was being done Mr. Heron arrived on the other side, two of his large dogs flanking him. He sized up the situation and as the dogs rushed forward at the figure hanging on the wire, he picked up a stone, threw it

26

at them and then used a piece of stick to drive them back. The two persons holding on to Nickar let go and ran a little distance away. The man cutting the fence also fled.

"Mr. Heron, sir ah know what you t'inking, but ah beg you sir, since it happen aready, ah beg you sir jus' let we get him off an' see if we can get him to the hospital cause him almost dead aready an' it no mek no sense you put yourself in any trouble." It was Mrs. Harmond begging, pleading, her voice rising hysterically and teetering on a wail.

He looked at her without speaking. She presented a pathetic figure with her tie-head askew on her head and her eyes filled with trepidation. These people are really vermin, he thought, they would be better off in another world, in another place. But, he reasoned to himself, as much as he could remember, she was not really a big problem; it was mainly other members of her family who were the problem. A tinge of sympathy touched his heart and he looked away from her to the people standing by hopefully. "Try get him off my property an' when I come here tomorrow make certain that the wire mend back!" At the sound of his shouting, the dogs got excited and again he drove them back with stones and a stick, making his way behind them. He did not look back.

They took Nickar to the village square and Godfrey's taxi, 'Betsy Dear', took him to the hospital. He was unconscious for three days because he had lost so much blood. A pall of fear and doom hung over the family and was only lifted somewhat when news came that he had regained consciousness and was talking a little.

From that day on Nickar was known as 'Baab Wire' behind his back, because no one dared called him the name to his face.

He also walked as if he were pressing the pedals of a bicycle or bike, and also got the name 'Pedal'.

Nickar had come from the hospital and a number of family members gathered at Gully Deep to find out how he was and to boost Mrs. Harmond's heart. His mother had called from abroad to speak to him but he refused to take the call and almost used obscene words to his grandmother and aunt when they tried to force him. Who was she anyway? He had no mother and if anybody was his mother, it was his grandmother.

Most of the family sat outside in the half moon which threw indistinct shadows all around and caused some members of the family to visualize things which existed only in their minds. One claimed that he saw a willowy lady dancing non-stop beside the kitchen; another insisted she had seen a man grabbing at a woman. To pass the time they sang folk songs and told stories. Mrs. Harmond's son, Markdon, led the folk songs. The third one was 'Sammy plant piece a corn down a gully an' it bear till it kill poor Sammy, Sammy dead, Sammy dead, Sammy dead oh, Sammy dead, Sammy dead, Sammy dead oh!'

While the song was being sung, Nickar called Mrs. Harmond. "Mama a whose nine night a keep? Why you have all this singing roun' the place?" He shifted a little and sweat rushed to his forehead as pain poked him in his side and feet.

Mrs. Harmond went outside and told them that Nickar was having a headache and could not deal with the noise so they were to tone it down.

It was then that the story telling started. Jen told the first 'Big Boy' story. Once upon a time when Big Boy was in class it was time for spelling. When his turn came the teacher asked him to spell 'mosquito'. Big Boy became very upset and complained,

"Miss why you ask me to spell such a small t'ing like mosquito! Why didn't you ask me to spell something big like cow?"

Everyone roared with laughter at Big Boy's reasoning.

Nickar did not appreciate the crowd and its sympathy. He knew they were saying all kinds of things behind his back and calling him names. Well he didn't care what anyone wanted to say or think. He had already made up his mind about how he wanted to live his life and he didn't want them around keeping any vigil for him. He wished they would go home, especially Aunt Leila and her two children. Whenever someone came in to talk to him, he pretended to be asleep. He didn't want any lectures, the ones his grandmother had given him since he regained consciousness were enough. Hustling something that nobody wanted was not a crime to him. Those breadfruit would have stayed up in that tree until they ripened and dropped, and that would have been nothing to Bird. He had so much yet he always looked hungry as if his buxom wife ate all the food in the house.

He had a problem with people in society who had too much when others had too little. They certainly could not take any of the wealth with them so it was better if someone helped them to use it more profitably and enjoy some of it for them. Why should anyone work for hours for four thousand dollars a week when there was enough to go around? It was not strange that he was not the only one who thought like this, his brother Tyrone shared his views. He too hated the mass intrusion of the relatives and was just humouring them. But he wished them gone and encouraged his brother to pretend deep sleep, supposedly induced by the medication he was taking for the pain.

He did this and to their relief by eleven-o-clock they were all gone but he had not seen the end of relatives. He refused to lie in bed the following day and went to lie outside under the almond tree on a tired, old lounge chair and who should come walking down the hill but Shanae, Michanne and Elton's sister, who lived in the city. She was very tall for her eighteen years but her supple movements enhanced her height as she moved like an athlete. Her winsome smile spread across her smooth, dark face and revealed her even, white teeth.

She had a suitcase and a handbag with her. Nickar had not seen her for two years and did not mind her or the visit. He was only piqued at the thought that she had come because of his so-called misfortune. He also had a second thought about the bulging suitcase; something about it suggested permanency.

Mrs. Harmond was extremely glad to see her granddaughter. She was very fond of her. Her bearing somehow reminded her of her daughter when she was a young woman. When she arrived she sat outside beside Nickar enjoying the cool breeze, as she said. She looked up at the screeching of the disputatious birds who were carrying out their favourite past time. Above them the john crows kept their circular movements as if they were waiting for the quarrel to become more than that and lead to a killing, and then they would swoop down. Shanae did not like them, they gave her a queasy feeling.

Michanne kept hugging her sister. "Model, what do we owe this pleasure to?" she asked, beaming at her.

"Well," Shanae started, looking away from everyone. "Ah just taking a break from the city for a while. You know cooling out, letting my hair down, getting the smoke an' the noise out of my system for a while. Ah might even see if ah can find a job for a little while you know, until I am ready to go back." She finished knowing that all the querying eyes were on her.

"But what about Miss Levi, she know you plan to stay away so long from town?" Mrs. Harmond asked. Miss Levi was the lady whom Shanae had been living with since her mother had migrated.

"Well, she can stay!" Shanae expostulated. "She kept on mumbling and grumbling about how much money my mother send, how often she send it an' how much she owe her. I really can't take the drop words so I leave to see if ah can get a job up at Merry Ville." She paused and then she went on, "I am eighteen now an' ah have five CXC subjects so I am going to look a job. Don't worry, as soon as I find my footing ah will leave down here and rent somewhere. I really don't want to create any more problem cause I know how the space go already." She finished and looked away in the distance, hoping that no one would question her.

"Well you know you always welcome here. If you not happy in town, it don't make sense you tarry there. We just have to see how this work out," Mrs. Harmond responded, giving her a welcoming smile. She did not want to betray the sudden sinking feeling that had been born in her belly.

The next night at about nine-o-clock there was a knocking on the door and when Jen opened it she saw Tyrone, Melvin, Austin and Elton. She hissed her teeth and closed back the door. "You ever see poppy show, since when them four come a knock on the door, wonder what game them up to? Let them stay out there." She then went and sat beside Shanae on the little bed in the living room. "Continue from where you did stop, cause I don't know what trick them four up to." Again, she hissed her teeth.

The knock came again and then Tyrone came in and called Mrs. Harmond. "Mama, somebody outside to you."

"To me at this time a night? Is what happen now? Ah hope none a you go out on the road go get into trouble cause I not going there!" She was emphatic and her face showed her determination.

"No Mama man nothing nuh happen. You a behave jus' like the people in the district. You t'ink every turn we turn we must be in trouble!" He looked at her as if she had no right to even think of any trouble related to them. "Just step outside Mama an' you will see who I bring to see you!"

Mystified, Mrs. Harmond stepped outside. She looked from one grandson to the other and then she saw the strange man. At first she did not recognize him but from somewhere in the deep caverns of her mind, the face surged up and she attached a name to it. For a while she opened her mouth but no sound escaped. She was simply speechless, a frozen figure, or one carved from the most solid material.

It was he who spoke first. "How you doing Sister Harry? Long time, as a matter of fact years since ah last saw you." The Jamaican accent, corrupted by the English accent, burst out in the silence of the moment.

Mrs. Harmond, as if awakened by the voice, placed her arms akimbo and stepped back. "Alabaster? Alabaster? What you doing in Jamaica? Something must be wrong to bring you here!" She stressed the 'must' and at the end of her exclamation, peered closely at him. The verandah light was off and she went inside and turned it on as if she did not trust the full moon which had exposed everything about the figure properly. She peered at Nickar and Tyrone's faces. The only differences were the age and the look of one thawing out after being frozen for too long. His face was puffy and wet even though it was not really hot. The resemblance between the three frightened her, and the commonly held belief that if the boys resembled the father they would be unlucky, and if the girls resembled their mother they would also be unlucky came to her. Intense foreboding gripped her. She could not understand this because now she could shift some of the responsibility from her shoulders to his. No sooner had the thought been born than she knew it was only fanciful thinking because Alabaster never stayed in one place too long. In addition to this, he did not really care for his children so what was he doing here?

She voiced the question again. "What you doing in Jamaica an' especially roun' these parts? How come my daughter never tell me you comin'?" Disbelief and suspicion were registered in her voice. She did not like the antipathy which his presence concretized. She had never approved of the fleeting relationship between him and her daughter. When she had heard they were living together abroad, she had never believed it.

For the third time she asked, "What you doing roun' here?" She turned to Jerome and asked, "Where you find him?"

Before Jerome could answer, Alabaster flagrantly said, "Somebody give me something to deliver for them and it turn out it was illegal."

"What you mean illegal?" Mrs. Harmond interrupted sharply.

"Well it was drugs," he said unabashed, "and it was a set up too. As soon as ah reach the place police arrest me and I spend one and a half year in prison and then them deport me." He looked at Mrs. Harmond and the boys without even one blink.

Well this one shame tree dead, Mrs. Harmond mused, a deportee!

"Well, Sister Harry you look shocked but even though ah haven't been round for a long time ah still remember the children. I hear Nickar sick so ah come to look for him." He was peering into the house trying to locate his children.

"Well ah really don't know what is going to come of this but ah hope now you will play a part in your children life an' set them straight." The hope in her voice sounded contrived and strained.

She moved aside for him to enter the house noting how dapper he looked; expensive-looking close fitting jeans, a red polo shirt which held on closely to his body, high-end tennis shoes and low cut hair with each obedient strand in place. He was Tyrone all over or Tyrone was him all over. She sat on the hard, wooden verandah chair out of the way of the meeting and greeting. She wanted to have nothing to do with it. "Tomorrow ah will call my daughter and ask her 'bout this," she planned. "How come she never even call an' say anything?" She realized she was talking to herself and stopped, then she said loudly, "God you know."

When the people in the community heard of Alabaster and Shanae's arrival, they held council.

"I don't t'ink it going to come to any good!" Green lizard commented. "When ah was in England I hear that him did join with some people that was no good! No good! Them behaviour was suspicious and them always in a wranglings with the police. Since I left there I don't think him change!" He tapped the shop piazza with his walking stick, emphasizing his point and glad that he had something to tell that the others might not have heard.

"Well," said Maternity who was sitting on the piazza, "with the curse that them curse with them no need no more bad luck roun' them. Ah hope the granny nuh allow them to be too much with him." Maternity's given name was Timothy Archer but everyone called him Maternity. He usually worked as a watch man at a brewery and he was often absent from work and so had exhausted all his leave. One day he went to his supervisor requesting more leave. The supervisor told him he had exhausted all his leave and jokingly added that the only other leave he could get was maternity leave. To the amusement of the company, later that day Mr. Archer applied for maternity leave.

"But she can't stop them. You no see all a them wayward already! She can't rule them! Them too much fi her an' on top of it see one next pretty little one gone down there to live. All a the bwoy dem bout the place jus' a eyes her off," Mr. Amos commented.

"She really look good but why she really left town an' come here? Ah would really want to know. She need a better place than that cursed gully!" Green Lizard posited.

Mr. Laza just sat and listened to it all. He did not feel like commenting.

Robbery At Church

Mrs. Harmond hobbled into the churchyard just as the worship service was beginning. She knew she was a little late but she lived a good distance away and she was not one of those that had a ride to church. She had not been for the past two weeks and was very happy she could make it. Being out of the house was a welcome escape from the arguing, the strains in relationships, the over-crowding and the poverty. She often found great relief in singing and shouting, it helped her to forget her troubles. She didn't mind being called an escapist. Sometimes she really felt that escaping from life was the best thing but could life really be called life without challenges?

When she got inside 'The Way To God', she sat at the back of the church. The front pews were for the righteous and the rich; she did not qualify. As she took her seat a number of eyes pinned her down and raked her from head to toe; from the old, clean, black straw hat with the ring of flowers, the blue and white poplin dress one of her daughters abroad had sent her, that almost covered the thick, brown stocking which gave way to the well-worn, well-polished, black pumps which bore dirt and white dust, the testimony of the long walk from Gully Deep to Harlington. As soon as they had inspected her clothing, their attention was riveted to her face. She was sure that she imagined the barbed looks and some tinged with astonishment, and she wondered what she or her accursed family had done now. People had been a little kinder when Rita had died but the accusatory stares of some had returned after Nickar and the breadfruit incident.

Mrs. Harmond decided that despite the arctic blast in the middle of summer, she was going to do what she had come all that distance for, worship. And worship she did, singing lustily, clapping loudly and shouting hallelujah. She even kicked a few dance moves and contorted her body when the spirit touched her. Those close to her watched curiously, whispered behind their hands and shook their heads in disgust. If Mrs. Harmond was aware of it, she did not give the slightest indication. She had learnt to be a duck, water on her back was of no account, she was schooled in shaking it off.

When the parson took the pulpit, the ugly glares made sense. He took his text from the commandments and it would not be fair to say he did not expound on each, but he did a command performance on stealing.

"Stealing to many has become a way of life. It has become the lifeline of those who refuse to follow the word of God and eat bread by their sweat!" He wiped the sweat from his forehead as he said the word.

"My God, hallelujah!" shouted Miss Ermine with her garish voice. She was sitting at the front of the church but she turned around for effect.

The parson continued, "Stealing is an abomination..."

"An abomination!" shouted Miss Ermine, repeating and stressing the word for the parson.

"It is an abomination and only evil and dishonest people practise it. If you follow the word of God you can see what happen to people who t'ief. They are cursed by God! They never come to anything but turn a murderer and an outcast, their whole family is cursed straight down to the last generation! I can tell you that. Look at Ananias and Sapphira, look what happen when they t'ief God tithes! They both drop down dead, dead! The one or ones who broke into this church and steal the fan, the polisher, the music boxes and most of all the week's tithes and offering will be cursed forever!"

"Forever!" bawled out Miss Ermine.

"Will be cursed forever right down to the last generation and beyond that," the pastor continued. "It has happened already and it will happen again! God is not a person to joke with!"

"Him is more than a person, Him is a being with punishment in Him hands!" Miss Ermine bawled out. Punctuating the parson's speech was not enough to get the message of the curse across, so Miss Ermine started a circuit around the church, wheeling and turning like an oscillating standing fan. Before you knew it, other people joined her and they all circled like hawks getting ready to swoop down for a kill. They did swoop down and perch at the back of the church where Mrs. Harmond was sitting. She sat immobile and watched as they circled her, all but one, Sister Esther Wright who stayed at the front of the church encircling the pastor's mother who had been sick for years. She could hardly walk and groaned intermittently, but when asked where was hurting she did not know and the doctors did not know what was wrong either.

The sisters encircled Mrs. Harmond and shouted in tongues. All eyes were on them as they performed in the spirit. Later on the story was told how she didn't even blink or twitch as she was beaten and chastised spiritually for the sins of her father and her children's children. They all but hit her, as she sat with disbelief engraved on her face. She did not leave the service until it was dismissed with prayers offered up for the individuals who were facing challenges in one way or another, and this included the parson's mother and his sixteen year old son who had not been well since the night before and had been showing little interest in church.

When the service was finished she greeted those nearby and went outside. Only Miss Lattie, her friend for years, sought out her company and consoled her just as she was leaving.

"Sister Harry ah bear with you, cause ah know that you are a decent God fearing and law abiding woman. Even if any of you grandchildren involve in anything ah know you don't sanction it cause you not that type. Don't let anybody prevent you from serving you God. One day, one day Him will grant deliverance and everything will be revealed, everything!" She shook her head and hugged her, much to the annoyance of some of those standing by.

Mrs. Harmond felt like a dog who had been offered a bite of food after it had been beaten and chased away. She had no idea that the church had been broken into and that even though no one had seen the perpetrators, her grandchildren had been blamed. Even if she had known she would still have attended church, as opting not to would have been tantamount to having knowledge of the crime and hiding to conceal her shame.

She sang for most of the way home: "Rock of ages cleft for me, let me hide myself in thee." When she got to the top of the hill, she stopped and looked down. She had been living in this place forever and she had nowhere else to go. Life had always been this way: poverty, babies and deception; she had had to live with the ethos of the community, the people would not let them be even when they themselves had similar problems. Their challenges and conflicts were relegated to the bizarre, obeah or coincidence; hers were as a result of a curse. If her family was so cursed then why didn't the church that she had been a part of for most of her life help her to remove the curse instead of helping the unrighteous to prey on her? This question had long been on her mind.

When she got to her house she sat on the bench under the tree. Immediately Jerome came out to sit with her. He was the only one who ever went to church with her but had decided not to go this particular Sunday. The other boys were gathered around the old, wooden table at the back of the kitchen playing dominoes, while the girls were engaged in hairdressing. Jen was just finishing with Shanae's hair; a long black mane floated down her back. Why did this girl who had so much hair of her own feel that she had to look like a horse, Mrs. Harmond questioned inwardly.

"Mama, you look sad, church didn't nice today?" Jerome asked, edging closer to his grandmother.

"Nice enough except for the murderation!" Mrs. Harmond sighed and shook her head.

"Murderation, is who dead?" Jerome asked, shocked.

"Ah didn't say anybody was dead. Ah talking bout how people keep on preaching on me when ah don't even know when you all doing wrong things." She looked at him searchingly.

"Wrong t'ings mama, you know I not mixed up in anyt'ing wrong cause I 'fraid! Moreover some of the things that people say we do down here is not true!"

"Well Jerome ah really can't swear for anyone, but ah really hope that this one not true." She raised her voice to the sharp peal of a bell and called, "Nickar, Tyrone, Shanae, Melvin, Austin, Elton, stop the everlasting knocking this big Sunday and come let me tell you something." Her voice had the 'I'm not in the mood for the foolishness' tone.

Everyone she had called came over to where she was sitting, looking at her in an annoyed manner.

"Is what happen now Mama, just as ah ready to murder the boy dem you call us." Nickar hissed his teeth irritatingly.

"You better mine you manners boy cause it don't matter how long you live you can't be as old as me! Moreover respect due even to me who curse and live down a Gully Deep." She glared at him and for a while Shanae thought she was going to hit him. Nickar did not flinch, he just glowered at her in return. Yes, his grand-mother was the only person he had ever come close to loving but he was not going to allow her or anyone else to hit him; no way.

Mrs. Harmond looked at Nickar and the unsettled feeling she kept having about him deepened. With his hair growing further and further away from his head and looking like a soursop, he looked terrifying. His shorts, which were heading for his shins, did not do anything to improve his image. Mrs. Harmond shuddered as if someone had walked over her grave spot, but she was going to say what she had to say.

"Which one of you break into the church an' t'ief the fan, music box an' the tithes an' offering?" She looked from one to the other.

42

Everyone burst out laughing except Nickar and Tyrone.

Melvin was the first to speak. "Mama, it look like you join up with the people in this God-forsaken district. Everything that happen is us down by Gully Deep. What happen to all the other t'ief them roun' the place?"

"Well you just say it, everything happen is you boys from down here an' since is so everybody believe ah have to ask the question." The pain which had been a permanent fixture in her eyes shone out.

Jerome looked at his grandmother and saw the pain. Empathy tugged at his insides. It was not fair, he reasoned silently, that his grandmother should have to raise so many of them and continue the life of anguish she had endured before them. It was just not fair.

Nickar and Tyrone walked away, halfway towards the table. Tyrone turned and shouted in the middle of denials from the other boys, "Let one a them come down here come search for anything an' them will see! Just let one a dem come down here!" He stormed after his brother and took up the dominoes, ready to start the game again.

"But what is this though! I didn't even know say them bruk the church! When them do it Mama?" Elton asked.

"It look like is Friday night. Ah wonder how come Brother Gustus never reach over here to spread the news an' drop him words?" Mrs. Harmond said aloud.

"Cause him not there," Simone offered. "Yesterday morning when ah was coming from shop ah see him an' him grandson, Timmy, going into Road Hog taxi."

"But this family is really bad luck, how come people just say is you when they didn't see you?" Shanae wanted to know.

43

"Well for one, yes we get mixed up sometimes but is not all the time. Sometimes things not nice down here and we might do a little wrong thing, but is not like how people let it sound. And the next thing is that from me have sense they keep on saying that we curse. How can we come out to anyt'ing when everybody expect us to do bad and wash them mouth on us all day long?" Melvin said, sitting on the ground beside Jerome.

"Let me tell you something my grandson," Mrs. Harmond said. "The thing to do is to shock people, if they expect bad, shock them with good. Let them eat their own words!"

"But how we mus' always do good when things so bad with us? So much people to eat and little money to buy food, no good place to live, nothing at all goin' for we!" Elton exclaimed.

"Well, you need to get education and leave this place. Find a job, that is the solution," said Mrs. Harmond. "But nobody want to go to school an' that is the way out. Ah talk day, ah talk night an' nobody not listening so don't complain!"

"We not to blame," Austin said, sitting flat on the ground and then lying down using his hands as a pillow. He watched the black birds and the crows circling overhead. The black birds competed to be heard, pecking furiously at one another, involved in their own private quarrel. "We not to blame," he repeated, hissing his teeth. "How come everybody else have mother and father and we don't have any?" He looked to the sky as if he hoped the answer would be displayed there or the birds would somehow include it in their squawking.

"I wouldn't say you don't have anyone, it's just that your parents have to seek life elsewhere. Things in Jamaica hard, especially roun' here where the only t'ing to do is farming—"

"But nothing not in farming, everybody roun' here plant little something for themselves so nobody not really buying unless is something scarce. The only thing that have a little money in it is weed," Austin put in before his grandmother could finish.

"An' you know jus' like me that weed is illegal! If it never illegal no money would be in it. An' not only that, it cause people to lose them head, look what it do to Mr. Myron boy, Keon! Good good boy turn idiot cause him won't leave the weed alone." Mrs. Harmond cast a warning look at Austin.

"Well Mama, people have to live, an' if is so them have to live, them have to live. Sometimes you have to try a little thing for youself, a so mi see it," Melvin said.

"Well hustling an' that ganja business both wrong an' I don't condone them kind of behaviour. Curse or no curse I not a thief or a wrong doer an' ah hope nobody in here don't mix up in the church breaking an' ah hope nobody down here don't get themself mix up in anyt'ing illegal or you on your own." She looked at each of the boys in turn and they looked back at her without saying a word. She then turned and looked at Shanae. "Shanae ah want to talk to you about something after dinner so don't bother to leave the yard like ah notice you start doing."

After dinner, a not so pleased Shanae sat on the bench under the tree waiting for her grandmother. She was dressed and ready to go on her walk to the road as she always put it. She looked at her approaching grandmother with pique as she had a very good idea of the sermon she wanted to preach to her. As she got closer, Shanae's irritation changed to sympathy as she detected the lines of strain and stress sculpted deeply into her grandmother's face. The deep roots at the corner of her mouth seemed to be increasing and had become more prominent since she had come to stay at Gully Deep. She did not want to be at Gully Deep but where else could she go? She would just have to stay there until she got the job she had been promised.

Her grandmother sat beside her and looked her fully in the eyes. "My granddaughter," she began, "don't take what ah have to say to you any way bad. You are my daughter child an' ah love you just like ah love my daughter." She paused and a faraway look stole into her eyes. She was probably reliving fond memories of her daughter. Shanae averted her eyes but she continued, "Shan ah want you to look at me an' listen to what ah have to say. Ah don't mean no harm but you need to think bout what you doing. Every day you get up an' go away an' ah don't really know where you go. You are a stranger to these parts an' you really don't know the people an' their ways so you need to be careful."

"But Mama don't you remember that ah told you that I'm looking a job?" Shanae seemed surprised at her grandmother's words.

"Yes, but people don't look job in the night an' most time you come in here late! Ah really don't understand that." The concern in her eyes heightened as she probed for a veracious reply.

"Honestly Mama, ah really looking a job an' I'm very close to getting one now." A look of relief surfaced in her eyes. "By this week I will know for sure," she said reassuringly.

"What kind of job you talking bout child?" Mrs. Harmond pressed her, wanting to get the details.

"Well ah not sure yet." Shanae seemed hesitant, vacillating about whether she should divulge any more information.

"How you mean you not sure? You must have an idea what kind a job you getting!" Mrs. Harmond demanded.

"Well, it have something to do with clothes. I might help in a clothes store or something like that." Her voice had a dubious quality about it, but she looked her grandmother in the eyes.

"Well that not too bad but with your subjects you could find something better in the nearest town. It would be a good thing if you could get to go to a college like you cousin, Laurine, but a guess you need to start somewhere. Anyway ah beg you, don't stay out late an' if you have to be out on the road late call one of the boys to come an' meet you."

"Yes Mama," she answered quickly, wanting the conversation to end so she could get away.

After she went back to the more youthful and lively company of her cousins, Mrs. Harmond sat and thought about the conversation. She didn't feel comfortable with the information and she had a disturbing feeling which was not only due to Shanae's hesitancy, but she could not identify what was causing the unease that was stirring inside her.

Leila's Visit

t was six months after Rita's death and again the family was gathered at Gully Deep to keep vigil. It was not a remembrance for Rita, nor a gathering to keep Nickar's company; it was a vigil that was held every year on this specific date, January the thirteenth, and it had been going on for thirteen years. As a matter of fact, family members were not the only ones present. People from Top Road – the area of the district above Gully Deep – also came to view the phenomenon and then discuss it the next day, adding succulent bits to the story and subtracting the parts that were not juicy.

Jerome was fourteen years old. January the thirteenth was his birthday, but instead of celebrating his birthday on that date or becoming involved in some joyous activity, Jerome was always sick. It started when he was actually one year old. By now everyone in the district knew the story. Jerome was one of identical twins who had been born fourteen years before. His twin brother, Jermaine, had only lived for six weeks. The doctors said he had somehow developed meningitis.

Jerome was left all alone and apart from ordinary common ailments, was physically fit most of the times. It was the most uncanny thing that on his birthday he always fell ill. From as early as minutes past twelve, as the thirteenth of January arrived, he would suddenly develop a raging fever and would start to thrash crazily around and writhe and cry in agony all day until the new day started. As he grew older the cries turned into a mournful monologue in which he beseeched someone or something not to take him away or stop pulling him under. For the first three years his mother had rushed him to the hospital expecting him to die, but miraculously when the new day started the fever would drop suddenly and he would become well in a matter of hours.

No doctor could explain this strange malady. They could find no cause for the frequent frenzied contortions and the intense fever which ravaged the small, pitiful child. After the third year, the family did not take the child to the doctor anymore, but kept their own vigil. Nobody really knew how the diagnosis was made but soon it became public knowledge that the dead twin, Jermaine, was the problem. He was lonely and wanted Jerome to come and be with him and so he tried as best he could every year to steal his brother. When the diagnosis was made those in the community who professed to have knowledge of the supernatural advised the family to make a life-size wooden doll and place it in the coffin. The supernatural pundits also advised that the doll should resemble the twins closely. Ras Carver was given the job. If anyone could make a true likeness, it was he. When he was finished those who saw the carving marvelled at the likeness.

The next problem was to get the doll into the coffin. It was not enough to put it into the grave, it had to be placed beside the skeleton remains of the deceased twin. The only way to do this was to dig up the grave and open the coffin. Only three family members volunteered to do this task. A few other people went along with them but kept their distance, fearing ghostly repercussions. Nothing out of the ordinary happened until they had covered the grave. As the three men were moving away, one suddenly fainted. The others who were on the periphery looking on ran away, leaving his two companions to carry him home. He remained unconscious for about an hour and just when they were contemplating taking him to the doctor, he suddenly sat up and asked where he was. By morning the community heard that the duppy had boxed down Milton.

The following Sunday, the pastor blasted all the people who delved in witchcraft instead of believing in the true and living God. He intimated that no wonder some people's lives were the way they were because all they ever did was heap curse upon curse.

Everyone thought that Jerome was delivered but the next birthday the same thing happened. People's view was that the deceased twin had not been fooled because the likeness should have been at the baby stage when the deceased twin died. People didn't grow older when they died, they remained the same so the deceased twin did not recognize the three-year old resemblance and so it had not worked and they knew it wouldn't have. Mrs. Harmond hissed her teeth at the foolishness and said she would have no more of the rubbish. Whatever God wanted to happen would have to happen, she didn't want anyone to put any more curse on the family.

After the failed attempt, every year the family and those who cared to, would gather at Gully Deep hours before Jerome's birthday and start the vigil which was closely akin to an exorcism. They prayed, sang, rebuked and read psalms. Then there were those who mopped Jerome's face and rubbed him with bay rum as he kicked, snaked into different wriggling positions and shouted to an unseen being.

"Let me go, ah not coming with you! Lawd Jesus, you smell bad, let me go! Leave me! Come out a me!"

Mrs. Harmond's daughter, Leila, was always present at the vigil. Although she did not visit Gully Deep often, she always contributed whatever financial aid she could to her mother. According to the people in the community she was the only child Mrs. Harmond had who had 'held up her head' or who had evaded the curse. She was an accountant in a reputable firm in the nearby town of Varston and had two children, Alston, age nineteen and Laurine, age seventeen. Alston was presently a sophomore in university majoring in computer science and Laurine had just been accepted to teachers' college. Leila was also married. Her husband was a bus owner and driver who took day students to the two boarding schools and another high school in the parish. They lived about two miles from Mrs. Harmond and very often escaped the lambasting levelled at the rest of the family. There were a few people living close to her who knew her family's history, but she kept her distance and pretended not to pick up the sarcasm hurled at her whenever anything happened back in the community and then winged its way to their area.

She was happy for her children that she had not chosen to migrate and cause their lives to fall apart. The children too were grateful that they were not in the thick of things, but they had not escaped all together as a small number of children from Harlington attended high school with them. When Rita had died, one girl had pointed her out at school in the lunch room and within her hearing, she had related not just Rita's death but what she had heard about the curse to everyone within earshot. Laurine had turned her back and looked into emptiness as if she was not the target of the report. When the teacher on canteen duty had stepped in to ensure that the lines were maintained and the talking kept at a minimum level, she had stealthily escaped, not wanting herself to be more obtrude.

Later at home, her mother had reassured her that there was no such thing as a curse and that all families had their problems, it was just that some people had a little more than others as a result of certain circumstances. Her mother assured her that such foolishness had nothing to do with her and that she should concentrate on her school work and do her best to strive in this challenging world, especially coming from her background.

As usual, Jerome survived his mysterious malady, but after he came out of it, he seemed weaker than he normally was. He was dazed and disoriented for a few hours and was quiet for a long time, just staring vacantly at nothing in particular and nodding to queries made about his health rather than vocalizing.

Leila wanted to talk to her mother about a matter so she stayed after the crowd had left. Before she could get to talk to her, she came across Nickar, Tyrone and Melvin sitting in the living room. She greeted them. "Hey boys, how is everything going so far?"

"Well nothing new, everything the same as usual, just looking at you the better one," Melvin answered, surveying her from head to toe, the relaxed, reserved features that never gave anything away, the bright, black eyes that saw more than they would acknowledge, the firmly set lips that could flare in fierce anger when the occasion arose. He also took notice of the expensive wedding band and the skirt made of fine fabric.

Leila observed the look but pretended not to see. "And you Nickar and Tyrone, how you doing? You didn't answer me. You looking more and more like your father." She smiled at them, encouraging speech.

Nickar gave what could only be described as a smirk or a near snarl, and a grunt of recognition as he shook his head.

Tyrone was a little more civil. "Hi Auntie Leila," he managed with a smile that barely widened his lips.

Leila looked at the boys and refused to let them ruffle her relaxed demeanour. "I see you have something against me, I wonder what that is now?"

"I don't have nothing against you Aunty, ah jus' watching you flourish and all that," Melvin said as he tried to joke off the boys' frigid attitude.

"Flourish, how you mean flourish, what makes you think that?" Leila looked from one to the other, trying to ignore the feeling of unease that was threatening to overcome her.

"Everyt'ing jus' nice and easy like cheese for you, the curse don't seem to bother you at all. Children bright and doing well, good job, good husband." Nickar finally spoke, the bitterness un-bridled, unsheathed, had escaped from him.

Leila looked at the boy, his hair like porcupine quills pointed in all directions. She could hear the bitterness and understand the sense of abandonment, but felt he had no right to aim it at her. "My children are bright and doing well because they go to school and work hard. I am trying to live comfortably because I worked hard and borrowed money to school myself when my mother never had a dime. I decided that I was going to fight against this so-called curse and make something of my life, not to get pregnant and to keep myself down and then blame it on a curse. Your mother, as a matter of fact, my sisters, decided to do something else – migrate. That was their decision, not mine. They were supposed to help you to be better off so don't blame me." Leila did not raise her voice, not once, even though she could feel the anger stinging her lashes. She was not going to allow her nephews to goad her to tears.

"Well, since our people nah sen' on the money, you need to leggo some a yours so we can live big too," Tyrone said with a laugh, and looked slyly at his aunt.

"Yes send a message and remind me to give you my pay cheque the next time." The sarcasm spilled out sharp and cold. Leila was not finished yet. "Why you don't ask mama how you eat here most of the time? Why you don't ask her that? If your parents were helping as they should mama would be better off. I could even take her to live with me." The placid look on her face belied the deep resentment inside her. She was getting tired of sporting a façade of nonchalance when it came to her mother and her siblings' children. After delivering her last statement she simply walked off and left them to stew in their envy and bitterness. As she walked away the thought came unbidden that she should warn her children to be cautious around them, especially Alston, who was very unassuming and got along well with everyone.

Her mother was sitting at her favourite spot, the bench under the tree. Everyone had left by now and the grandchildren were about their business so she had only the garrulous blackbirds and the ever circling carrion crows for company. Leila noticed her drained, stressed face and asked herself the question she had asked an infinite number of times, why didn't they change the law to make it illegal for children to burden their parents after they had already struggled to raise their own. They should only raise grandchildren in the event of death or extenuating circumstances.

Her mother saw her approaching and made space for her on the bench. Leila sat beside her and held her hand in a friendly manner.

"Mama how you really doing? I don't like how you look so tired and drawn. You need to come by me for a little while and get some rest," Leila coaxed.

"Lee ah would love to but you know how it go roun' here." She shrugged her shoulders forlornly, registering the futility of the situation.

"Mama, you don't have any baby down here, everybody is big man and woman," Leila countered.

"That's true, but ah have to keep the peace an' see to it that things share right an' run the best way it can down here," Mrs. Harmond replied.

"And talking about peace Mama, what else gone wrong round here? Melvin, Nickar and Tyrone were very rude to me, it was like they want to blame me for their problems. How I get into their life I don't know." Leila could feel the anger building up again.

"Lee, you know that anybody at all that is in this family get pull into everything whether they want to or not."

"But Mama, look how much time I help you out so that they can have something to eat! I wonder if they think is their parents send most of the little money that feed them down here?" Leila was getting more annoyed by the minute.

"They very well know, cause I not ungrateful an' ah always mention it. They very well know, especially the boys them, ungrateful an' trouble making." Mrs. Harmond was becoming as angry as Leila. "Them getting worse an' ah really don't know what is happening cause when ah ask everybody ignore me."

"How you mean Mama? How you mean you don't know what is happening?"

"Lee girl, ever since Nickar an' Tyrone father come them start staying out extra late an' ah hear them go town several time. When ah try to question them, ah knock my head into a stone wall, nobody pay mi no mine. An' the next t'ing is that Melvin, Austin an' Elton start get up early a morning an' coming back home late evening." Mrs. Harmond looked at her daughter searchingly as if she could supply some answers.

"Mama, none of what you are saying make any sense but I think they are involved in something, I don't know what. Ever since I heard that worthless man, Nickar and Tyrone father is back in Jamaica, and is a deportee, I know something bound to go wrong, cause he never mind them when he was out here and then all of a sudden him come around here all friendly! That man spell trouble! Look how the boys get facety like wasps out for revenge." As Leila spoke, all kinds of unpleasant images raced around in her mind. She did not know what to make of them; she did not want to put them into words or keep the pictures active.

"Leila, ah call Markdon an' Tobias to talk to them but when Tobias come Nickar play like him want to fight him an' Tobias get ignorant an' tell him if he didn't behave himself, him must leave down here. Nickar tell him that nobody can move him from here until him choose to. When Markdon hear bout Nickar behaviour him refuse to come down here cause him know that him would kill him if him touch him an' ah really glad him never come." Mrs. Harmond ended the story and sat back looking hopeless and fatigued.

Leila's heart ached and inwardly she called her siblings all kinds of derogatory names and derided them for neglecting their filial duty towards their mother and causing her so much pain. She wanted to take away her mother immediately but she knew she would not come. She changed the topic to the one she wanted to discuss, Shanae. "Mama, I really want to talk about Shanae."

"Shanae, Lawd, she is another worry. Ah don't know what to do about her." The worry lines on her face deepened as she shook her head.

"Mama, I really want to help her. She has a good brain and if she get some help, she can really come out to something. I took it on myself to talk to the principal of the same college Laurine is supposed to attend September and he said I could take her for an interview next week." Leila looked hopefully at her mother, glad there was at least one good thing to report.

"God, ah hope it will work out Lee. I don't know if she want to go that way. You will really have to talk to her. Moreover, where she would get the money from?" Mrs. Harmond turned to her daughter with an enquiring look.

"Well Mama, I talk to Humphrey about me borrowing some money to help her and he said I could go ahead. If she gets through, I will let her share a room with Laurine." Leila sounded excited.

Mrs. Harmond was excited too. "Lawd ah jus' hope she go along with you, it would make her more stable an' make something of herself. Ah would stop worrying about the late nights an' that job ah not certain about at all. Shanae! Shanae! Come here now!" Mrs. Harmond shouted. "Shanae! Shanae!"

Shanae came at a half run. She had been in the house talking to some other relatives. Her attractive face had questions beaming all over. The long horse mane was flopping at the back.

"Yes Mama?" she said, approaching warily and looking from one to the other.

Leila made room for her on the bench. "Sit down Shanae, we are not going to eat you."

Shanae sat and her aunt told her about the plan. She listened without interruption, keeping her head down. When her aunt was finished she said, "Aunt Leila, I thank you for thinking about me but I really not interested in teaching."

"You have the ability, you would do well," Leila coaxed. "I really want you to become something worthwhile."

"Yes Aunt Leila and I really thank you, but I am not cut out for the classroom. I prefer business, selling and working with people, not children." She sounded sure about what she wanted.

"Yes, Shanae, if that is what you want to do fine, but you need to get a good background and then you can branch off. Use education as a stepping stone." Leila was all persuasion and passion, but Shanae looked apathetic and unconvinced, and shook her head repeatedly.

"Well, if you don't want to go to teacher's college, maybe you could do some business courses at the community college. Maybe some accounts, economics and so on." Leila was not giving up.

"Yes that sounds better but ah taking a break from books right now; but in the new year if you still want to help me I would be very grateful." A little interest had seeped into her voice.

"Alright, I can't force you," Leila said in a tone tinged with surrender. "To each his own. Next year I will still help you, but in the meantime be careful."

The birds who owned the property equally with Mrs. Harmond started a racket overhead. They all looked up and saw two black birds pecking at each other purposefully. Shanae got up and threw a stone at them and they flew off in a huff, still screaming at each other. After they flew away there was still some noise. Mrs. Harmond recognized it as the steady drilling of a woodpecker making inroads in a tree with its sharp beak. She ignored the annoyance as it was something she had become accustomed to.

Shanae seized the opportunity to sneak away. When her aunt and grandmother sat down again she had vanished like a spectre.

EEE

It was Christmas Eve and Mrs. Harmond was all alone except for Jerome. Everyone else had gone about his or her business. The boys did not disclose their destinations but the girls claimed they had gone shopping or to a dance of some sort. The children's parents had sent a little money and they were using it on themselves. Mrs. Harmond noticed that of late Nickar and Tyrone were cooking all types of expensive meals and buying all kinds of designer clothes. Her queries as to the source of the funds had yielded two words: my father. Mrs. Harmond had not seen him since the night he had surprised them with his presence and she was glad, but the boys seemed to be meeting him somewhere.

Having finished her chores for the day, Mrs. Harmond went and sat under the tree. She had only the black birds and crows for company. The circling, diving and chattering went on relentlessly even though it was time for them to retire for the day. Mrs. Harmond ignored them and paid attention instead to her environment.

Jerome had white washed the tree trunks, something which was done yearly at Christmas and they looked different, dressed in their white socks. A small plot of sugar cane growing nearby nodded sleepily in the lazy wind, their white and brown flowers accentuating the white tree trunks and giving a kind of eeriness to the tired sun which was showing its weariness by withdrawing its glow and leaving only a swathe of bright orange and purple. It shed a bright but cold light in the east. In the west a few grey clouds had congregated and they scowled with disapproval at the bright straggling clouds, willing them to be on their way so that the dusk of evening could descend upon the earth and take its rightful place in the order of nature.

Jerome came outside and sat by his grandmother. She was grateful for his company even though she wished he would be more open and social. It would appear as if his unusual condition had affected all aspects of his life. He lived in fear of his birthday and the pain and agony he had to suffer on that particular day. In his heart he felt that one day he would not make it. He had confessed his thought to his grandmother and she told him that the will to live sometimes exceeded the power of medicine. Medicine could not help him but if he resisted the urge to give up and was determined to fight, he would live and could one day defy the demons who wanted to determine his destiny. Jerome had become so timid that he often backed out of arguments with his siblings and cousins, especially Nickar and Tyrone, who were not just unfriendly at times but actually teased him and called him a sissy when he obeyed his grandmother. They hated the fact that he had continued going to school after his grandmother begged and pleaded with him.

He decided not to go shopping or sightseeing or whatever the others were doing, claiming that he had done what he had to do already and did not wish to join in any festivities. Even though Mrs. Harmond was glad that he was not in the company of the other boys, she wished that he would go out and enjoy himself.

As Jerome sat down Mrs. Harmond turned to him. "Jerome from morning ah don't see Shanae, when the others was leaving she was not with them, an' ah don't think she working today. How come she lef' so early?"

"Mama she come in early this morning bout one-o-clock an' then by five-o-clock ah hear the door opening an' when ah peep outside ah see her almost running up the hill. I don't know where she gone so early." Jerome looked at his grandmother as though he expected her to have the answer even though she was the one who asked the question.

"Well ah tired of talking to her about the time she come in here. Ah tremble every time ah think of her walking in the dark passing all those bush an' gully an' God knows what." She looked out into the encroaching dusk and then turned her attention to the belligerent birds. They were going home for the night but not without announcing their departure with loud, discontented and argumentative cries. The woodpecker had ceased hammering its beak into the mango tree, but the crows continue to circle over-head like red-hat foremen overseeing closing down activities.

It was then that they heard voices and running feet coming down the hill. Mrs. Harmond was surprised that any of the grand-children would be returning home so early. She thought that maybe they wanted to bathe and change, and then disappear until Christmas morning, but why were they running?

As they got nearer, Mrs. Harmond heard what sounded like bawling. She got up and turned to Jerome. "Lawd, ah feel sick all of a sudden, from morning ah know that something wrong! Lawd help me to bear whatever it is." She sat on the bench and Jerome sat beside her and held her hand.

Jen, Joan-Ann, Austin and Michanne burst into the yard like a freak storm and made straight for her. Jerome held her hand tighter in his sweating one; his heart was fisting his chest viciously.

"Mama! Mama! Oh God Mama!" Jen bawled, falling to the ground as her knees lost the ability to function. Michanne dropped beside her and held her belly and bawled loudly like a cow in distress.

"Oh God! Oh God! Lawd Father, how we going to bear this!" Joan-Ann covered her face, sat on the ground and then removed her hands and started beating the ground.

It was Austin who broke the news to the two sitting in shocked silence. "Mama Shanae! Mama Shanae!" He was stuck at the two words as if he were singing a song and those words were the only ones in his repertoire. "Mama Shanae! Mama Shanae!" His voice sounded hoarse as one unused to emotion.

"What happen Austin? What happen, talk nuh." This came from Jerome who had released his grandmother's hand and was now standing.

Encouraged by the prompting, Austin said, "Mama Shanae dead! Shanae dead!"

"Boy stop you nonsense! Today a Christmas Eve not Tom fool day! Don't make them kind a joke, you a idiot or what!"

"It is not a joke, Mama," Michanne said, holding her knees and rocking to and fro like an off balance rocking chair. Streams of tears coursed down her face unhampered.

"What you mean Shanae dead?" Mrs. Harmond's voice, small and distant, came at them.

"Mama we went into town and was doing little shopping, walking around and enjoying ourself when we hear people screaming an' running over to the place behind the market where them kill animal. We ask two people what happen over there and them say them find a body over there. Me and Michanne go over there but the crowd so big that it take a good time to get to the front. When we fighting to get to the front we hear some people say a big van drive pass on the road and throw the body off and speed weh. At first, them never know it was a person, them t'ink it was rubbish but somebody go roun' there and find out that is a human body." Michanne stopped talking and started beating the ground with her fist. She was sobbing so loudly that she was unable to speak.

Jen continued the relay. "When we get to the front, the first thing we see was the new skirt and blouse that she buy last week and say she was going to wear today. When we run up to the body is Shanae! Jesus Christ is Shanae! Somebody kill her and throw her weh like dog!" Jen got up and walked backward and forward, holding her head and stomping her feet.

Mrs. Harmond sat trying to figure out if she were alive or not. She could still hear and her heart was bursting with silent fright so she must be alive, but her senses were numb, frozen to be exact. She could not think, speak or move, she just sat there and everything seemed so far off and surreal like she was watching one of those made up movie things that everybody knew was just for entertainment.

She was jerked back to the present when a weeping Joan-Ann said, "Some police coming down the hill and Melvin coming with them."

Mrs. Harmond sat immobile as the mountains. She did not turn to watch the police advance, neither did she hear the last squawk as the birds went off for their night's rest.

Three police officers accompanied by Melvin entered the yard. They were young men and looked like they were newly weaned from their mothers. They looked about them curiously, fascinated by the topography of the place, the seemingly carved out, sloping hills covered with vegetation and farming which led straight down to the level area with the small, old-fashioned house and the tiny outhouses. Their eyes strayed to the barbecue which had gungo put to dry on crocus bags. Then they looked at the little group of mourners who eyed them with unwelcome stares.

"Good evening," the trio chorused, looking from one person to the other, not sure how to begin even though it was obvious that the news had preceded them. "Are you Mrs. Harmond?" the one at the front asked, looking at Mrs. Harmond and trying to maintain an unwavering and professional gaze.

Mrs. Harmond nodded without answering. She had temporarily lost the ability to talk, speech eluded her like she was a stone figure.

"Mrs. Harmond, we are very sorry to officially inform you about the death of your grand-daughter. It is a very terrible thing to happen to anyone, especially one so young and promising as we have heard she was. I sincerely hope that God will give you and the rest of the family the strength to bear up. The police will try to do everything we can to find the person or persons responsible but we need all the help you can give us. We will not trouble you tonight because we know how you must feel, but we are asking you and any member of your family who might be able to help, to come to the station tomorrow morning." He paused after the long, rehearsed speech, glad to have reached the end of the unpleasant undertaking.

Mrs. Harmond tried to answer but only a low grunt came from her. She nodded a mechanical response instead. The young man proferred his hand and Mrs. Harmond extended hers, and he shook it.

They left but not without looking too keenly at the grieving girls. They were wearing body hugging stretch jeans and equally tight sleeveless blouses which did not require the imagination to do any work; everything was fully displayed. The looks did not escape Mrs. Harmond and a slight tremor shook her body as she remembered that this was the way Shanae usually dressed even when she claimed she was going to work.

The police officers took their leave and as the evening advanced, more and more people made their way to Gully Deep. Brother Gustus was the first to arrive and for once he sat quietly without his usual spiky comments. Shanae had not really grown up there and even though people had a poor perception of the family, that did not stop them from coming to express their condolences and at the same time try to find out what had propelled any human being to do what he or they had done to the poor girl. Even the pastor, his brother Harold and his oldest son came. They mingled with everyone and even indulged in swapping murder motives. The pastor's brother, a tall imposing figure with a full moon face, two owl-eyes, a brown goatee beard and huge cartoon hands, proposed that the girl must have fallen prey to someone who had offered her a lift or someone she might have become friendly with, and knowing some of these men they were only out to have a good time. Almost everyone agreed with him, advancing or altering few changes to his theory.

Mrs. Harmond sat and listened to them all. She did not move from the bench at any time. She was inert, except for her eyes which wandered from face to face. She listened without showing that she was. The popular opinion was that she was in a state of shock and should be watched carefully.

The Funeral

The following morning, Mrs. Harmond, Jen, Michanne, Joan-Ann and Melvin made their way to the police station. Leila and Laurine were waiting there for them.

The police disclosed what they had found out. Shanae had been stabbed several times and then thrown from the back of a black F150. No one had seen the driver's face as the vehicle was heavily tinted and had barely paused. The police theorized that someone else who was in the vehicle had pushed or thrown her outside because the driver would have had to stop longer to do that. He must have been working with someone. The autopsy would give more details of how she had died.

Mrs. Harmond and her family were questioned about Shanae's activity in town. Only the girls had any information to supply and it was very little.

"Where was she working?" the officer in charge of the case asked.

"I don't exactly know," Michanne said, "it had something to do with a clothes store but she said that she was going to leave that an' go into modelling."

"Modelling," the officer repeated.

"Yes Sir, she said that someone was going to help her get into it," Michanne said.

The police officer wrote swiftly and then responded, "There is a modelling agency somewhere in town so we will check that. Did she say who was going to help her with this job?"

This time Jen answered. "She said her friend was going to help her."

"Friend? What friend?" the officer asked.

The girls looked from one to the other and then at Mrs. Harmond without answering.

"Girls, what friend?" the officer prompted with impatience in his voice, looking from one to the other in a meaningful way.

"Ah don't know him," said Jen quickly. "She only said her friend would help her."

"I don't know him either, she only said his name is Cleveland and that he was a big man," Michanne said, looking away from her grandmother's accusing glare.

"Big man how?" the officer asked.

"She said him big and tall and that he was much older than she." Michanne seemed to be the one with most of the information.

"Did she tell you where he was from?" the officer questioned, anxiously feeling as if he was getting somewhere.

"No, she only say she meet him in town after work and that him drive." Michanne supplied information again.

"Drive what?" the officer asked, getting ready to write.

"I don't have a clue," Michanne answered.

"She never really want to say much. It look like it was kind of a secret friendship."

"Do you have anything more that you want to tell us about Shanae's clandestine relationship?" the officer asked, promising to keep them informed as the investigation progressed.

No one answered.

When they went back to their community, everyone gathered around them hungry for information but they had none. They themselves would have been glad to be supplied with some, but all their ears were fed with were speculations and the news that some of them knew that something bad would happen because a pretty girl should not have been seen coming home late at nights by herself. Moreover, she should have remembered that her family was 'bad luck' and she should have been more careful. Mrs. Harmond listened to it all without responding. She noted the avoidance of the word curse and the change to 'bad luck' and she thought that they were trying to be kind because of their bereavement. When they were on their way to Gully Deep she started to sing *What a friend we have in Jesus, all our pains and grief to bear.*

Gully Deep was alive with activity. It was as busy as the street on a major market day. Mrs. Harmond was kept busy for most of the day, helping to make plans and overseeing them. Her family gave full support to Shanae's parents who had come for the funeral. Mrs. Harmond was overjoyed to see her daughter, but lamented the fact that it was death which had compelled her to visit. Mrs. Harmond secretly watched her daughter and concluded that things seemed to have gone well with her. She still looked young and attractive and it was not difficult to see Shanae in her, down to the very gait. She moved adroitly despite her height and the forced smile which infrequently emphasized her dark, smooth, attractive face drew glances from many.

It was only early morning that the family was left by itself and it was on the third morning that the tightly reined in emotions exploded. Since their parents' arrival, Michanne and Elton had been coldly polite to them. For the most part, they had avoided them and spoke to them only in the presence of others. They refused to call them mummy and daddy and if they had to address them, they would go only as close as was needed for them to hear and then address them without the calling of names.

On the third morning Mrs. Harmond asked Michanne to tell her mother that she needed to decide who was going to write and read the eulogy.

Michanne stood at a distance which she presumed she could be heard from and said, "Mama say you need to decide who is going to write and read the eulogy."

Michanne's mother was sitting on the verandah talking to Leila and did not respond. Thinking she had not heard, Michanne went a little closer and repeated the message.

"Michanne who are you talking to?" Leila asked.

"Well is not you Aunty Leila." She turned and started to walk off.

"Michanne." Leila's cool yet cutting voice riveted her to the spot. "Does your mother have a name and a title? Don't you think that some amount of respect is due?"

"What you expect me to call her Aunty Leila?" Michanne turned at half angle and stared into her aunt's face.

Undaunted, Leila held her glance. "A simple mummy or mom will do."

"Mummy! Mom! That is what people call their mother. The only mother I have is mama."

"I brought you into this world," her mother said, turning to look at her at last.

"Sure it's you. You brought us in and you left us in it all by our-self!" The subdued anger had risen, Michanne was finally getting her case heard.

Elton who was standing nearby walked over to give evidence in the court hearing. He looked at his mother as one who scorned putrid garbage and lashed out at her. "Is because of you why Shanae dead!"

His mother, Annette, looked at her son's angry face and became petrified at what she saw. "How come I am responsible for Shanae's death? I wasn't even here." Her defence was lame, a confirmation of what had gone wrong. Realizing how her very words had betrayed her, she looked away into nothingness.

"You more than right!" Elton continued to attack. "You go way after you done breed up the unwanted dog puppies! You go way an' leave them on poor mama an' anybody else who would take up you mistake dem. If you had looked after you pickney dem like a mother, Shanae would be alive today! Not dead, butchered like hog by some murderer like you." He was shaking with anger and Mrs. Harmond who had approached at the sound of the angry voices had never seen him cry before, but there was Elton crying away, his shoulders heaving rhythmically to the song of pain in his heart.

Everyone had gathered around by now and it was Melvin who pulled him away and disappeared into the bushes with him. Mrs. Harmond held on to Michanne's hand, urging her to stop being rude, but Michanne pulled away from her gently and continued her assault.

"From you lef' the dog puppy dem an' go about you business an' promise how much you going to take us over there not even one of us don't move an inch from this gully bottom! You hardly send anything for us cause you expect mama to t'ief to prevent us from starving! You cause Shanae to die! Why you come out here? Who want you out here? Go back where you come from! Your hand them free, you nuh have no responsibility! Why you come out here any at all? Go back where you come from!" She started bawling, sounding like a cow who had bellowed herself hoarse. The tirade had taken a toll on her voice.

Mrs. Harmond wrenched her away, remonstrating her for lambasting her mother. She led her inside her bedroom and closed the door. She spoke softly at first and then as the sobbing subsided, she spoke harshly to her. "Mich ah know you hurt, every single one of us hurting an' what you say might have a little truth in it but you really can't blame your mother for everyt'ing, no girl! Remember that your Aunt Leila try to get Shan to go to college but she never go! Memba say Shan make up her mind about what she want an' yes if her mother was around it might have prevented her but you an' me don't know that." She tried to hug her granddaughter but Michanne broke away and ran towards the door.

"Mama, even dog and wild animal need their mother! Everybody deserve to have a mother. She could a send for we, or even come look for we, even one time a year. Look how long she over there and is the first time she come out here and for what, to ease herself of part of the burden permanently; one of the dog puppy dead!" She wrenched open the door and ran out of the house with Jen, Joan-Ann and Simone in tow.

Michanne and Elton's father were not present when the blame game was being played out, he had gone to see his parents in another parish. The children's mother, feeling threatened like an animal targeted for a hunt, packed her suitcase and swiftly made her escape. Word came to the family that while she was fleeing in a taxi, it overturned because the driver who was trying to escape from the police because of unpaid traffic tickets was driving recklessly. Annette was thrown from the vehicle when the car hit the embankment but luckily for her, she sustained only a broken arm and some scrapes to her face and neck. The community's response to this was that the accident was in part a punishment for Annette and a continuation of the curse. She received very little sympathy from the young people of Gully Deep. Elton was overheard to have said, "Good fi her, should be she instead of Shan."

On the day of the autopsy, again Mrs. Harmond was the only one brave enough to go inside although quite a few family members were gathered outside. The autopsy revealed that Shanae had been stabbed three times and that she had been two months pregnant at the time of her death. Mrs. Harmond almost fainted at the sight of her granddaughter, the pretty girl lying there dead.

When Mrs. Harmond went outside, she again kept the last bit of information to herself. There was no need to give rise to more speculations and analysis of the family. She would ponder these things in her heart and when she was good and ready, she would deal with the ones she could.

The funeral turned out to be a grand gala. Mrs. Harmond was certain that only a small percentage of the people, pushing and shoving like bulldozers, knew Shanae. Experience had taught her that large crowds did not flock funerals unless one was a celebrity, an extremely popular person, a philanthropist or had died under tragic or mysterious circumstances. The manner in which Shanae had died was both tragic and mysterious and so had it been a movie, she would have been a box office hit. People from neighbouring communities had also heard about the curse on the family so they wanted to see the family for themselves. They asked anyone they could to point out the members of the family and repeated bits of the information they had gleaned in the hope that more would be added to it. In that way they had enough to go back and report to those who had been unfortunate to miss the grand event.

The young men from Gully Deep, with the exception of Elton, stayed outside the church. They kept themselves away from the crowd like mere onlookers and so they were easily pointed out and their history recited to the ravenous newsgatherers. In the church, Mrs. Harmond sat at the front with Shanae's parents and her daughter Leila and her children. Shanae's mother, Leila and all her female members of the family wept copiously. At one point the preceedings had to stop because Michanne had started up a sound like an engine whistling along a railroad track. It went from a low note to a piercing peal and no one could hear what the officiating minister was saying. His wife, who was sitting on the choir, discreetly requested that she be placed outside for a while but she roughly pushed away Joan-Ann and Laurine who undertook the task. Laurine almost fell and had to grab the bench in front of her for support. In all of this Mrs. Harmond kept quiet, singing her own song silently. Her emotions and tear-ducts seemed to be suffering from drought even though all around her it was raining tears.

The message was more like an onslaught of words directly aimed at young people. Their stubbornness, lack of good manners, indolence, sinfulness and all the negatives one could think of were highlighted and attacked. It was pointed out that the young were a generation of vipers as substantiated by the scriptures and if they did not follow Christ they would all like-wise perish. The church was on fire in support of the preacher. Looking on, Elton visibly shook his head in bewilderment because some of the supporters were known sinners. Their behaviour cemented the opinion he generally held of most adults: they had unwritten laws for themselves, and they did not remember that it was their bad examples that the young people mostly followed. There seemed to be one Bible for them and one for the young people. He did not heed the pastor's warning to come and be prayed for, or face eternal damnation.

No sooner than they reached Gully Deep for the interment, the rain started. Some people were soaked and closely resembled rats who had been thrown into the river, but they would not miss the finale of the grand gala for anything. They stayed huddled like packed meat under the tent which had been erected in the front yard.

The rain did not last long and they made their way to the graveside, gingerly trying to evade puddles and slippery areas. The pallbearers were in front bearing the coffin when Michanne dashed from the house and pushed her way through the crowd like a worm tunnelling its way through mud. To the anger and astonishment of the people, she stepped on them and pushed them aside unceremoniously. But worse was to come. She ran straight into the pallbearers, knocking one end of the coffin from two of them. She fell into the mud and so did one of the pall-bearers. The other one fell right into the grave, pulling along some of the sodden mound of earth with him. He had fallen on his side and the earth started covering him.

"Lawd Jesus, the wrong person a get bury!" Who Dat bawled out. "Man stand up quick before you get stifle!"

75

"Somebody get the ladder quick, quick!" Maternity bawled out. "Get the ladder!"

Elton quickly got the ladder which was leaning on the ackee tree and dropped it into the grave. The frightened pallbearer climbed up quickly as if something was in the grave pushing him up. At that point everybody started to laugh and cheer. Things soon got back to normal and all the rituals were performed and the corpse intended for the grave was interred. Michanne became unusually quiet. Jen and Joan-Ann stuck tightly to her like limpets, but that was not necessary. The tears had abated and she stood like Lot's wife throughout the whole thing. Her mother was the one who did the crying this time, wailing like a woman in travail, only she was not bringing a child into the world but ushering one out. Her brothers held her closely and as soon as the singing stopped, they led her away into the house.

Nickar watched the people heading for the tent where the food had been served and was placed in boxes. He knew that was what some of them had come for and also to gain fodder for gossip. He hated them all and wished that as soon as they ate the food they would just drop down and expire. All these 'wanga gut' hypocrites who had stuffed their bellies the night before at the wake and had come back again. He had left the wake as soon as they started the fearful din of clashing the pot covers and slurring the songs like they had speech defects. Left to him, Shanae's duppy would have wandered around the place until eternity before he would hold a wake to entertain and feed all the sanctimonious two-sided machetes who had found their way to Gully Deep. Planting her was enough to keep her still; they had not needed a wake. They were now jostling each other for food from his family, the cursed people. Nickar wished that the so-called curse could be transferred through the food. He hated them all. He took one final look at the Philistines, hissed his teeth and walked up the hill and away from Gully Deep. Tyrone saw him leaving and knowing what the problem was and that he shared the same opinion, he followed him.

Michanne walked into the living room where family members were sitting. Her mother and father were sitting in the corner around the small table. Her mother's head was down and her shoulders were heaving. Her broken arm was resting conspicuously on the table. Her husband was trying to console her. No one saw when Michanne moved, but as swift as a thought, she was in the corner. She took off her shoes and hit her father in his face, and before he knew what was happening, she had hit her mother on her head twice before he grabbed her, slapped her across the face and shook her.

"You little wretch, how dare you? Don't let me have to damage you this evening. Who you think you hitting?" He pushed her away roughly and sent her sprawling to the floor.

Elton rushed from the doorway where he had been hovering like the birds who lived on the property before Michanne came into the room. He stepped over Michanne and grabbed his father. It was then that the real fight started. They both got in some good hits before other family members managed to pull them apart. One of Elton's eyes was shut and blood dribbled from under the eyelids. His father's jacket was hanging in pieces and blood zigzagged down his nose and stained his blue shirt. Already his face had started swelling.

Everyone outside was trying to get into the living room. For the moment the food was forgotten and so was Michanne who was lying on the floor. She had tried to get up but had fallen back, rendered weak by the searing pain in her head. She had knocked her head when she had fallen on the floor. She started groaning in pain, opening and closing her eyes and groaning lowly. The crowd in the living room started waltzing in dizzying time before her eyes. Soon they became a mass of dark confusion and then faded into black nothingness.

It was Mrs. Harmond who had managed to push her way into the room during the fight who saw Michanne on the floor.

"Move from her, move from her!" she screamed to those who were too close or were trying to make their way to the scene of the action. "Move from her, move from her! Mine you trample her!" Mrs. Harmond shouted, bending over Michanne and flailing her arms to keep away intrusive feet from the still body.

"Jesus mercy, how she jus' lie down so!" one of the persons nearest to her gave out.

"It look like she not breeding!" said another with concern mounting in her voice.

"But is how she get pan the floor?" another asked, looking around begging for an answer.

"Give her some hair. Give her some hair!" another shouted.

Those standing close by moved back a little but not too far back because they wanted to see what was happening for themselves.

"Michanne! Mich! Mich!" Mrs. Harmond called anxiously. Getting no response, she started to shake the inert figure vigorously.

"No don't do that you might cause further damage," a commanding voice said.

Mrs. Harmond looked up into the face of her pastor. The crowd had made way for him and he was standing over them. His brother stood beside him.

"Don't shake her," he repeated. "Somebody get some alcohol and smelling salts instead."

78

Jen pushed her way into Mrs. Harmond's room and came back with an almost empty bottle of smelling salt. The pastor all but grabbed it from her hand, hastily opened the bottle and held it to Michanne's nose. There was no response. He called her name over and over but nothing happened.

Despite the instruction not to shake her, Mrs. Harmond grabbed her hands and started shaking her. The pastor's brother caught her hands and held them both in one of his hairy paws. She looked down at the hand and then up at the face. She did not like the moustache which resembled the bristles of a worn wash brush. The hair covered a firm, sternly set top lip. The eyes were black and dead and Mrs. Harmond felt uncomfortable. Involuntarily, she released her hands from him and looked down anxiously at Michanne.

The pastor felt for a pulse and got one. "How did she fall?" he asked no one in particular.

Nobody answered and he looked from one face to another. "Well, she needs to go to the hospital because she is not responding. Maybe then somebody will tell them how she fell!"

"My car is parked at the top, I can take her," his brother offered. "Somebody help me to get her to the top and some family members will have to come with her," he added.

Mrs. Harmond and Elton volunteered to go with Michanne. When they left, Michanne's parents were just standing looking at their daughter being lifted away without them being able to accompany her or help in any way. They felt like strangers who had landed in an unknown place where in spite of their differences, they were still inconspicuous. As soon as the group had reached the top of the hill and had driven off, they quietly slipped away, pretending to ignore the gossip around them, but that was not possible. Their lives would never be the same again. Their experience was indelibly ingrained in their minds.

At the community council held on the piazza that night, the tongues clanged and bellowed out loud and long. Mr. Lazarus' shop was full and the crowd spilled out past the piazza and up and down the street. It was the same funeral crowd. Nobody had bothered to go home; they were still dressed in their funeral garb, except that the men had removed their jackets and the women their high heel shoes. They leaned against walls, tree trunks, sat on the piazza or sidewalk, or the men just simply stooped on their haunches or stood with their legs spread eagled, beer bottles, rum glasses and drinks container in hand. The street light glowered down upon them and further up, the unwilling moon pushed out its head shyly, overseeing the noisy activities of the night. It was Sunday night so the music was at rest and the voices flowed loudly on the cool night air.

"But my God what a thing! You ever see anything like this before?" The voice was high pitched and incredulous.

"Man, not in all my sixty odd ears on this planet earth," an equally unbelieving one responded.

"One murder an' then the same family member them almost murder another one at the funeral!" The speaker threw up his hands towards heaven.

"Good God, parents an' pickney a fight, first pickney attack parents an' the parents attack back an' nobody really know what really happen to the little gal. Jesus Father them people really curse in truth. Ah wouldn't want my dog to get mix up in that breed!" the first speaker commented.

"But is really a curse or is jus' bad luck them have?" a shy voice questioned.

"Bad luck or curse, whichever one you want to call it, something wrong with them. Daughter murder, mother han' bruk, children fight off parents, parents fight off pickney, you don't see that something gone really, really bad!" another bystander proclaimed.

"I don't know how truth it is, but me hear that the one that dead was along with a big man that married and have a family. I don't know how truth it is, but me hear that is the wife who set up the killing." The voice ended on a wavering note.

"But how can people know that when no one never really know who she was along with. I don't believe everything I hear. If nobody don't know who she was along with then how people know that?" The person asking the question stood up and threw it to all and sundry, but no one really knew.

"Look here man, you hear what black people say, if it don't exactly go like dat, it go near so! Don't tell me that nobody at all don't have a clue bout this murder!" a man leaning on one of the tree trunks said loudly, then unwound himself and stepped out in the road.

"Guess what, anything that happen in the dark, must come to light one day. I believe that. Everything must reveal cause Jehovah God not sleeping, Him no light no matches. Him no put on pyjamas." The predictor was a woman who sold baked products on the street and at the nearby market for a living.

"But Lawd Father, I don't understand—" started another by-stander, but she was interrupted.

"What you don't understand, something just wrong with the whole family!" The speaker was the person who had given information about the killing.

"Wait and listen, you never let me finish what ah was going to say. Ah wasn't talking about that." She paused and cleared

81

her throat. "I was going to point out how Sister Harry just take the whole thing. She just sit an' observe an' sing, not one piece a eye water! Is what make she?"

"Is true, when Rita dead, she stand up strong, now her grand-daughter dead all she do a sing an' look an' now one grand-daughter gone a hospital, an' she gone with her, strong as Jack Hammer ole donkey that him have for years now a walk miles a carry weight in a hamper going to market!" one woman exclaimed.

"Is the dead truth, but she is going to break down and lose her nerves soon, you mark my word. Nobody can't go through so much and don't even bawl one eye-water, it no natural," the speaker who had raised the issue commented.

"Despite what anybody want to say, I think that woman have a little good in her. Is God give her strength, not man and even if she give way she still strong, I couldn't deal with all this."

"Boy I just hope that the little one that gone to hospital don't dead cause that would be another attaclapse again." The speaker clapped his hands to emphasize the drama that would ensue.

Michanne's Predicament

Michanne was released from the hospital two weeks later. The doctors said she had hit the back of her head when she had fallen and that she had a concussion and was suffering from amnesia. When she got home to Gully Deep it was obvious that the problem was far more serious than the doctors had said or wanted to admit. Michanne did not answer to her name. When anyone called her, she made no indication that she had heard. If she looked around, it was not in response to her name but to a sound. She would sit in one place for hours, just staring impassively at nothing in particular and then she would get up and shout something incomprehensible. When questioned, she would continue her vacuous stare. Her eyes were glazed, huge and round, and threatened to fall out of their sockets. It was a task to get her to eat. Jen, Simone and Joan-Ann had to beg and coax her. Mrs. Harmond was the only one who could get her to eat freely and so the task fell to her. She was also the only one who could get her to bathe and comb her hair. She refused to take her medication, so Mrs. Harmond had to put it into her drink. Sometimes she would knock over the drink as if she knew what she was drinking.

She seemed to be suffering from severe headaches and when she was in pain, she would bang her head on whatever surface was at hand, even the ground. Then she would cry out "Pain, my head! My head, pain!"

When these occurrences took place, one or two family members would hold her until she quietened down. They were very gentle with her, even Nickar. When he was around he would sit and hold her hand and talk to her as if she were a young child who needed to learn the language. His now growing locks had given him a look of maturity and even though Michanne seemed to be far away, she also appeared to be listening to him.

Mrs. Harmond had taken to more singing and praying. She ate only enough to keep her bones and flesh from disintegrating. Her face had become strained and deep furrows had dug their way across her forehead and at the sides of her mouth. The few black strands of hair on her head were completely smothered by the dominant white ones. Her hair had become considerably shorter. It just seemed to disappear over the weeks, but like a rock, she remained grounded and unmoving. The troubles had only chipped away at her exterior; she appeared emotionally sturdy for one so old. Her voice rang out in daring defiance at the onerous task of living in her wide-awake nightmare. She refused to succumb to the quagmire of gossip and despondency that surrounded her and sought to choke her to tears and render her an ignoramus. The hard hammer of aging was also nailing her with arthritic pain and circulatory problems but she held her head up, not as a scornful stork, but as a watchful wren. Everyone spoke of her resilience and fortitude in the face of sickness and death.

Mrs. Harmond had not seen her only sister, Miranda, for over fifteen years. She knew she was living somewhere in Spanish Town but she did not know where, because her address frequently changed in the letters she wrote twice a year.

One week after Michanne had come from the hospital, she was sitting on the bench under her favourite tree listening to the birds' tirade. A baby bird had fallen from a nest and they seemed to be quarrelling about who had caused it and how to get her back into the nest. Mrs. Harmond watched the baby bird floundering in the grass. She was making pathetic peeping cries. A larger bird which seemed to be her mother flew down suddenly from the tree and perched on the ground beside it. She then encircled the bird making worrying, squawking sounds. Another bird flew down to keep her company and together they made loud, discordant sounds which reminded one of the musicians of Bremen. The racket attracted Mrs. Harmond's dog, Gypsy. He raced around the house side and headed straight for the birds, barking furiously, flaring his nostrils, baring his teeth and wagging his tail vigorously like a spectator shaking a flagstick at a sports meet.

Mrs. Harmond jumped up and chased him away. "Move dog, move Gypsy, go away an' leave the harmless birds!"

Gypsy, sad at being reproved, ran back a little and continued barking. He looked from Mrs. Harmond to the birds, obviously wondering why she was taking their side against him.

Mrs. Harmond shook her fist at him threateningly. "Gypsy move an' don't let me lick you today!" She searched the ground for a small stone and when she found it, she shied at him.

He looked at her in a surprised, disappointing manner like a child who had been punished unnecessarily, gave a lingering growl and then slinked away eyeing Mrs. Harmond all the time.

"Jerome, Jerome, come here," she looked towards the house and shouted.

"Yes Mama, ah coming!" he shouted back, running out of the house.

"Jerome take up that poor, half-dead baby bird an' put it back in the nest," she commanded, going back to the bench.

"But Mama suppose them other bird pick me?" he protested loudly.

"Boy you 'fraid a two little bird or the two little bird them 'fraid of you! Which one a them?" She hissed her teeth.

"But Mama you see how much a them up in the tree, especially the black bird them? Them certain to pick out my eye them!" He continued to protest as he took up the baby bird in his hands. As he started to climb the tree, Michanne came out of the house and stood under the tree watching him. Her hair was half combed and her eyes were lit with interest. The other girls had followed her out and stood by her side, not wanting to disturb or hurry her.

While they all watched, Gypsy started running up the hill and began to bark. He seemed glad to have found another diversion; he knew when he was not wanted.

"Joan-Ann, all of you better see who that busy body dog going after!" Mrs. Harmond shouted above the noise of the barking.

The girls started running up the hill shouting for Gypsy to get back but he continued his barking. At that moment Jerome had reached the nest. With much trepidation, he lowered the bird into the nest, not looking to see if he had put it on the other birds in the nest. He was counting his blessings and shinnying down the tree when three black birds, as if they had waited for him to complete his act of mercy, swooped down upon him and started pecking him all over.

"Jesus wooh, wooh God, same t'ing a did tell mama!" he exclaimed loudly, but he did not make the mistake of letting go of the tree to ward off the pecks. He jumped to safety and only then did the birds let up. Mrs. Harmond held her hips and laughed. The laughter rumbled from the depths of her belly and made its way to her throat. She convulsed in mirth as she saw Jerome fleeing down the tree in a comical way. She straightened up when she heard a laugh and felt a touch. When she looked up, she saw that it was Michanne. Mrs. Harmond did not stop laughing but simply hugged Michanne to her. It was the first time both of them were laughing in weeks. By now Jermaine had come down and his sense of humour caused him to join in the laughter. He sat down at the end of the bench and examined the small abrasions he had suffered from the birds' assault.

"Ah so happy to see you laughing," a voice commented close by.

Mrs. Harmond partially unwound herself from Michanne and looked towards the voice, disbelief washing over her face. She was glad for the opportunity of holding Michanne close to her, so she kept one of her arms around her while she looked at the person in front of her.

"Miranda! Miri! Bless my eye sight, where you come from girl?" Mrs. Harmond was beside herself with joy. She was laughing for the second time that day which about summed up the number of times she had laughed in the past months. "Miri gal where did you drop from? Jesus Saviour it has been years!" She released Michanne and hugged her sister tightly like a drowning woman clinging to a buoy.

"Lord Harry, ah so glad to see you, so glad! Lawd ah never know ah could be so glad to see anyone like how ah glad to see you!" She laughed in a high, squeaky manner like a mouse caught in a trap. Whereas Mrs. Harmond was a slight woman, she was buxom. Her large breasts pulled her head downwards and arched her back, but this did not impede her gait. She could stride forward like a boat which had set sail with her arms flailing like paddles. She had the same watered down complexion like her sister, but that was where the similarities between them ended. Her nose was wide and acted as a covering for the top lip which involuntarily trembled with laughter and usually spread to her owl's eyes.

"You come to look for me, mi sista." It was more a statement than a question. "Ah so glad to see you, but what bring you here at this time?" Mrs. Harmond made room on the bench for her. Michanne tried to move away, but Mrs. Harmond put one arm around her firmly.

Miranda laughed, squeaking and rasping as she did so. "Girl ah was in the market selling an' ah overhear some people talking about some t'ings that happen. The names that they call did sound familiar an' when ah ask them the name of the place an' them tell me, ah know it was you an' ah had to come." The laughter had disappeared from her voice and eyes; she looked first at her sister and then at her relatives who had come out to see who was visiting with them. They were making sure that it was not Mr. Gustus. They saw him as an old hypocrite and hated when he came to visit or more to the point, when he came to gather news to feed to the rest of the community. He had stopped coming for a while because of a name calling incident. The following day after the funeral, Nickar was passing by his house and took issue with his too inquisitive stare. Piqued, Nickar had shouted, "Rumhead

Hog!" – a long time name he had been given when he used to drink profusely. Mr. Gustus had shaken his stick at him and called him Baab Wire. Not satisfied with calling him a nick-name, Mr. Gustus tapped his way over to Mrs. Harmond's house to complain. After he had made his complaint, Mrs. Harmond called Nickar to apologize to Mr. Gustus. Nickar came forward at once and shouted to Mr. Gustus, "Gustus is who calling you out of you Rumhead Hog? Just tell me who calling you out a you Rumhead Hog." Mr. Gustus flung his stick at him, hobbled to retrieve it and then walked away cursing the whole family. Mrs. Harmond had not seen him since; everyone was relieved.

When they arrived at the seat, Mrs. Harmond introduced them. There were smiles all around. At least Miranda was not an outsider who had come to rub salt in their wounds about the curse, she was family, a new sympathetic face. She made herself comfortable, talking and laughing with everyone, deliberately skirting around the rumours, avoiding provocative questions and making everyone, except Michanne, laugh at childhood escapades and adult inconsistencies. Mrs. Harmond was more than unprepared for what happened next.

"Ah come here on a special mission," she finally announced.

"Special mission!" Mrs. Harmond exclaimed. "Is what dat now, ah thought you jus' come to look for us."

"Of course ah come to look for you, but ah also come to offer help cause you see me here laughing but my heart tearing out with what happening to my family. Ah come to tell you what to do to get this foolishness off you that is destroying you!" She spoke softly, reassuringly, without looking at Mrs. Harmond.

"Now careful now Miri, careful, you was always a hype up person. Don't bother put any kind of impossible idea into these young people head." She waved a warning finger at her.

Miranda ignored her and continued speaking. "Ah know that you are a Christian Sis, but at the same time God give you wisdom so you can survive in this here wicked world. Don't it Harry?" She looked at her, expecting the affirmative.

"Yes he give us wisdom but some people mistake what them want to do as wisdom with what God want them to do. The two is not the same," she said in a poignant voice.

"Well, be it so or not, we have to help ourself, especially us that everybody sentence to death an' put curse on. One day, one day, everything about this family will be revealed. What we guilty of will come to light an' what we are not guilty of will also come to light." Her voice held a note of warning.

"But Aunty what we can do to protect ourself?" Tyrone asked anxiously, pressing closely to his grand-aunt.

"Well bwoy listen, listen everybody, I know a man who can do things to protect you." Her voice became hushed and heavy. "Ah know a man who can give you all a bath to ward off evil an' a ring to wear to warn you when danger is near." She looked around her and got the hopeful looks she had expected from all but Mrs. Harmond and Michanne, who gave no indication that she knew what was being said.

"Yes, yes ah hear 'bout dem kind a people," Nickar said, getting excited. "Where is this person?"

Before she could answer, Mrs. Harmond spoke. "Listen, Miri don't bother with that foolishness. Don't bother full up the pickney dem head with foolishness bout bath an' ring. I know people who use their hard earn money an' do the same foolishness you talking about, an' them not one inch better, not one inch better. The family is already in trouble, don't heap down more of God's wrath on us. What must happen, must happen, bath an' ring can't stop that!"

As she spoke her face became red with passion. She looked at the faces around for understanding and support, but found none except a little wavering from the girls.

"Listen to me Harry, things can't get worse, accident, death an' everything else, you have to let the young ones protect themselves Harry! You have to stop the deading in the family! Too many people deading an' getting sick. You have to stop the curse!"

"Yes God will stop it when Him ready, since you t'ink is a curse, Him will stop it when Him ready. As for me, I am not going down to Egypt!" Mrs. Harmond said emphatically, stressing the Egypt.

"Egypt, which Egypt Mama? In all your life I don't think you ever go further than the nearest town much less Egypt!" Joan-Ann laughed out loud and then put her hand over her mouth.

"Chile you making a laughing stock out of me. If you don't understand something, the t'ing to do is ask." Mrs. Harmond turned to Joan-Ann and froze her laughter with a harsh look.

"Joan, to go down to Egypt mean to go to an evil place. It don't mean going to the country call Egypt," Miranda explained, looking at Joan-Ann. "Moreover with our poverty where would we get the money to go to such a place?" There was laughter in her voice.

Joan-Ann felt humbled and looked away from her grandmother's face. She decided that she would not say anything else for the duration of the conversation, but Nickar was not finished.

"Aunt Miri, tell me more bout this person, where mi can find him?"

"Where you goin' find money from to do this foolishness?" Mrs. Harmond questioned. "Ah hope you don't think I going to give you one cent, not even if I did have money walking on like dirt."

"Don't worry Mama, mi cool. Mi will find the money to protect myself cause too much people a drop out a dis family," Nickar announced.

"Nickar tell me something, what you protecting from? I been on this earth a long time now an' yes some people go an' get bath who not involved in anyt'ing at all cause them claim them warding off evil, but is only when people mix up in criminal activity that them wear guard ring." She looked searchingly at Nickar. "Tell me something, is which criminal activity you mix up in?"

"Mama sometimes ah swear you worse than the people roun' here, ready to suspect us of everything." He glared at her accusingly, rudely.

"Nickar, you don't need to talk to you grandmother like that. You must remember that she is more than a mother to you. Ah only making a suggestion, ah don't come to cause confusion an' disrespect. Respect is due." Miranda turned on Nickar sharply, her huge nose slightly flaring.

"You don't understand Aunt Miri, Mama always look at us jus' like her church people who really don't like her an' the rest of this community who even worse than her church. Ah really don't want to be rude to her but sometimes..." His angry eyes became dark and then it glowered with bitterness.

"Aunt Miri, jus' tell us how we can get to this person instead of this quarrel, quarrel. The fact is we need protection an' right now," Tyrone interjected, anxiety and hope surfacing in his eyes.

"Excuse me." Mrs. Harmond got up, holding tightly to Michanne hand. "Joan-Ann, Simone, Jerome, you better come with me. Ah don't want you taking part in any of this. Ah seem to have lost control of the rest of you. You mus' know what you want to do." She led the way, still holding tightly to Michanne's hand. When she turned around only Jermaine was following. The girls had stopped halfway. Mrs. Harmond opened her mouth to call them but thought better of it and closed her mouth.

Miranda spent two days and then she left. Since the grand-children were always going here and there Mrs. Harmond had no idea when the act was done but by two weeks later, she noted that all the boys except Jermaine were wearing strange rings. She pretended not to see and went about her business singing, her hurt submerged and a placid look seated on her face.

Relationships deteriorated in the house; the boys were obviously a team against Jerome. They had found ways of making money and he was not included. He didn't go off on the early morning jaunts with Melvin, Austin and Elton, but continued with his last year of schooling. Nickar and Tyrone disappeared sometimes for a whole day.

Jerome was often called names such as sissy boy and fish bait. Nickar told him he didn't have any gumption and that was why his duppy brother would finally get him. Elton wanted to know why he was still going to school as it would do him no good. Jerome told him that his aunt and her children were benefitting from education. To this Nickar laughed and pointed out that he, Jerome, was not in that bracket and that he should stop trying to get himself into the upper class.

Jerome did not let them daunt his academic pursuit. The fact was that he had somehow managed to keep his focus despite his strange malady and all that was happening to his family. His teachers were expecting him to do well and he intended to do so. He spent much of his studying time at school because of the situation at home. Mrs. Harmond's heart was never at ease until Jerome came home each day. She warned him never to allow dark to catch him on the road, and never to accept rides from any stranger. His cousins wanted to know if he was a girl and felt justified in calling him names.

Mrs. Harmond's Son Disappears

rs. Harmond had not been to church for a few months. Her arthritis had got the better of her and her left knee had become as swollen as a pumped up toy and had impeded her free movement. Most of the time she had hopped or hobbled around. She felt like a visitor as she walked into the assembly. Her face was serious and she held her head in front of her as straight as a pole anchored by mortar. She wanted to discourage questions and comments and be as inconspicuous as possible, so she sat close to the back in a corner to a window.

As she settled in, she felt uncomfortable. It was the odd feeling of eyes piercing into her, searching, probing and digging. She ignored it for a while but as the discomfort continued, she turned to see who it was. The discomfiting glare belonged to Mr. Bentley, one of the oldest persons in the community. He was eighty-five years old but seemed ageless. The wrinkles on his face were surface ones and his hair was grey instead of white, as one would expect at his age. His small, black eyes were piercing and vigilant. They darted everywhere and seemed to trap and assess everything before letting it go. The people in the community said next to God, he knew everything about what had gone, or what was going on, and what was to come in the community. This incredible feat was possible because he was the richest man in the community. He owned the largest property and had scores of cattle and acres of coffee. He also owned two haberdasheries in the parish which were managed by his two sons, Leonard and Carson. The people claimed he was white and called him Busha, but his mother was white and his father a fair-skinned Indian. He employed the largest number of people on his estate. He was always outdoors mingling with the workers even though he didn't really talk that much. He listened to every bit of gossip about the community people, asked very few questions and digested much. Many people found it strange that he attended an evangelical church when a Baptist, Anglican or Catholic would have better suited his personality and station. Even though he sang, prayed and read the Bible, he did not get himself involved in speaking in tongues or any other spirit related activity. When those activities were going on he just observed and kept a face as passive as a bleached stone. The word was out that his father had been special friends of the parson's father since childhood. His two children and four grandchildren did not attend the church when they were in the community.

Mrs. Harmond was not quite certain how she felt about this man. She had never spoken to him except for the customary greeting expected of Christians, even though she learnt that her father had worked for him for a while. He always shook his head in response to people's greetings and peered at them with his fathomless eyes as if they were objects of uncertain humanity and that was how he regarded everyone except the parson and his brothers.

Mrs. Harmond wondered what he was doing sitting at the back with the common people instead of the front section close to the door where he normally sat. She also wondered why she had piqued his interest so that he had condescended to stare at her. She fixed him with a glare that was far from being obsequious and then turned her attention to worship.

The parson did not seem especially fired up that particular day. He spoke mainly about overcoming the challenges of life, pointing out that they were necessary for Christian living. At the end, he begged for prayer for his family, especially his mother who was worsening and his son who was showing signs of departing from the faith. He said that the devil was seeking a foot-hold in his family but that he was determined to trample him.

While the parson was praying she thought about her own problems. If she had voiced them to anyone in the community they would have asked her what was different, she always had problems. The trouble was all the girls except Simone had stopped going to school. Joan-Ann had reached the school-leaving age even though she had not graduated because of irregular attendance. She did not attempt any of the school leaving exams and only showed interest in anything related to the care of hair. Jen still had another year of school but refused to attend because she deemed it a waste of time. Her specialist area was Home Economics but she showed no interest and often hid from the classes whenever she went to school. Simone, the youngest girl, went maybe three days for the week. Mrs. Harmond was not certain that she even went to school those three days. She often arrived home late in the evenings and cited no transportation to get to her community as an excuse.

Mrs. Harmond continuously warned her, reminding her of what had happened to Shanae.

Except for Jerome, school was history for the other boys. Mrs. Harmond was certain that Nickar and Tyrone were involved in something in town, while the other three boys were planting ganja somewhere nearby. She had seen though pretended not to, a few strange men in the vicinity of Gully Deep. She had wanted to investigate but her swollen knee had prevented her.

In addition to all these problems there was Michanne. Sometimes she seemed to have regained her senses fully and then she relapsed. Any kind of excessive noise and stressful situation would cause her to withdraw into the secret chambers of her mind. To add to that ill, her parents had stopped sending the little money they usually did. She had written her daughter a harsh letter but to no avail. The word was she was finished with everyone in Jamaica. Mrs. Harmond wondered how she could be finished when she never really started. She kept all this to herself, not wishing to burst open festering wounds and cause more pain. The boys did most of the cooking. They had moved from simple fare such as tin food and vegetable to chicken and meat. She inquired as to the source of the funds and was told they were now working. When she asked where, she got no answer. Mrs. Harmond warned them about illegal activities and told them she wanted no part of anything that they brought home. She also warned them about creating more problems for the family but this was greeted with grunts and silence.

After church some people seemed genuinely happy to see her out. She accepted their seeming solicitude, telling herself that if they wanted to be hypocrites, then that would be on their own consciences.

When she was almost ready to leave, she accidentally bumped into a woman. She said her excuses and on looking up, she realized that it was Miss Cathy. Miss Cathy was the woman that Pete had taken to live with him shortly after Rita died. Rumour had it that they had been having a clandestine affair while Rita was still alive. Like everyone else Mrs. Harmond's eyes quickly reverted to her belly to see if Pete was in line to get his most sacred wish but nothing was visible. Cathy followed Mrs. Harmond's eyes, hissed her teeth rudely and walked off, inwardly berating Mrs. Harmond and everyone else for their temerity where her personal business was concerned. Mrs. Harmond had seen Pete only about two times since Rita died. Both had turned in the opposite direction and walked hastily away. Mrs. Harmond's heart was quite sore and heavy with the secret she was carrying. When the time was right she told herself, some things would be revealed.

None of her sons or their children had attended church but as Mrs. Harmond started down the road, Markdon's neighbour, Miss Helen, shouted after her.

"Sister Harry, oh Sister Harry. Wait there one minute." She came up to Miss Harmond, gasping for breath. She reached into her handbag and pulled out an envelope. "Sister Harry, my Lord ah almost go back home with it. Never member a word bout it. Maas Mark ask me to give you dis. Ah sure him would kill me if ah did go back home with it!" As she rasped out the words, she stretched out her short, fat hand and handed Mrs. Harmond a small envelope.

"God bless you Sister Helen. Tell him howdy for me and that ah long to see him." She took the envelope and placed it inside her handbag.

"Ah will certainly do that Sister Harry and ah really glad you could come out today. You have to just keep on fighting."

"God bless you again, Sister Helen," Mrs. Harmond said and hobbled away.

When she got home, she went into her room and hurriedly opened the envelope. There was an untidy rectangle of paper wrapped around a five-hundred dollar bill. She hid the money and then read the note, partially vocalizing the words:

Dear Mama,

Ah have a little news about Shan death. Ah prefer to tell you myself tomorrow. Enclose find a little change.

Mark.

Mrs. Harmond's heart quickened and she sat on her bed with the note in her hand and then she read it again, peering carefully at each word as if she had never seen writing before. Finally she folded it carefully, put it back into the envelope and put it away in her bag.

That night, Mrs. Harmond slept fitfully. She dreamt that she was in a crowd and Shanae was trying to get to her but the crowd kept pushing her back. She stretched out her hands towards her, long, thin, shaking hands that soon melted into nothingness along with her face and form. She gave a cry and sat up in bed, not certain where she was. As soon as reality returned, she chided herself. The Bible said that dreams were as a result of a multitude of thoughts, and she knew she had gone to bed thinking about Shanae and the note she had received from her son. She could hardly wait to hear what he had uncovered.

She laid down and slept for a few minutes, and dreamt that she was again in the crowd but this time there was no Shanae, only some rowdy young men quarrelling with one another. Again she jumped up and sat in the bed. There were angry voices coming from the living room. Mrs. Harmond got up and walked hastily towards the living room. It was approximately twelve-o-clock and all the boys except Jerome, seemed to be just coming in from wherever they had been.

"Is a new day, why people can't sleep in their bed?" Mrs. Harmond shouted, walking into the living room. Her face was tired and drawn, and she kept opening and closing her eyes and stifling yawns.

"Why you don't ask you pet grandson?" Nickar said rudely, faking a smile which turned into a snarl, made more pronounced by the short, stubby new beard.

"Don't talk to Mama like that!" whispered Melvin loudly, jabbing Nickar with his elbow.

Nickar winced and glared at him. There was glowing anger on his face as he struggled to decide whether he should hit back Melvin or not. Melvin stood his ground and glared back at him, daring him to hit back. After a while, he hissed his teeth and looked away.

Mrs. Harmond watched the whole thing without commenting.

She again asked the question, "Why people can't sleep in their bed in peace?"

Jerome offered an explanation. "They want to beat me up cause I didn't wake up right away to open the door for them."

"Say that again, boy!" Mrs. Harmond stepped closer to the four-some as if she was going to hit them. "Since when Jerome turn door keeper for any of you? You act as if you own this place, coming in here every night late or before daylight. Nobody know where you coming from an' since you are Jerome's father him must sit up an' open door for you anytime you come in even when duppy an' dog 'fraid to walk! You see as of tonight, that not going to work anymore. Anytime you come in on time you welcome to come inside. If everybody sleeping nobody obligated to open any door for nobody. You better decide where you want to sleep." Mrs. Harmond was all fired up. "Ah been talking to you from a long time now about your schooling an' behaviour but you don't lissen, you don't pay me any mine. Ah hope when you get into trouble you don't look in my direction! Ah know that things an' time hard especially for us poor cast away people but it don't say you have to behave like you doing an' then because poor Jerome don't decide to go round with you, you hate him. Because ah don't say anything sometime you think ah don't notice how you treat him an' the names you calling him. But continue with you programme, you will see where it will get you! One day, one day you will remember what ah always a tell you. An' another thing, this little two by four belong to me, not any of you. Ah let you live here because of the kindness of my heart. Your parents leave you with me an' despite the problems ah still do my best. But guess what, ah will not get up an' talk every day, that is for young, strong people not an old, tired woman like me. Ah would like to get a little sleep an' ah don't want no noise inside here." She walked away and left them standing there.

Nickar was sweltering with anger, his Adam's apple was throbbing rhythmically and his eyes were like pointed knives glinting in the lamp light of the small living room. Jerome noted them and was afraid. He inwardly vowed not to get in Nickar's way if he could help it. His first step was not to sleep in the same room with him when he was angry. He sat on one of the chairs in the living room and that was where he spent the night.

Mrs. Harmond awoke with the feeling that her head was a pin cushion and that someone was busy sticking needles and pins into it. She ascribed the pain to lack of sleep as she had twisted and turned the whole night with images of Rita and Shanae, and someone who was always behind them in the dark chasing someone or something she could not see.

Mrs. Harmond did something she had not done for a long time. She took a painkiller and went back to bed in what she would refer to as broad daylight when everyone should be up and working. Jerome was gone to school and the girls were very worried. They kept going into the room and waking up Mrs. Harmond for one contrived reason after the other. They felt her to see if she had a high temperature and offered her coffee and porridge in bed. She was unused to such attention but sent them away telling them that they had disrupted her sleep the previous night, and she would be alright after she got a little sleep if they would be so kind as to allow her that pleasure.

Surprisingly, she slept for two hours and then she woke up suddenly and ran to the veranda calling out, "Jen, Joan-Ann, Simone, which day is today? Why you never wake me from morning!"

The girls all came running and laughing, glad that their grandmother was awake. "Mama you know how much time we try wake you from morning an' you run us." Joan-Ann was laughing hysterically. "Mama you getting old!"

"Leave me alone, I old long time an' except for sickness an' you slow down ah want you to tell me what wrong with it." Mrs. Harmond was giving tit for tat, trying to ignore the relentless pin pricks which were now a little closer to the surface of the cushion.

"Well Mama when you old you dead sooner or later," Simone said shyly, not wanting to upset her grandmother.

"Yes child but Rita an' Shan never old," she said quietly and looked out before her into nothingness.

No one responded and she went and heated up the breakfast she had been offered earlier and took her time eating it because her taste buds did not approve of it. She did a few things around the house, all the time keeping an eye out for her son but she knew he still had enough time to come. At about one p.m., she went to sit under the tree. The birds who had earlier taken a siesta woke up a few minutes later and without preamble, started their usual clamour. Mrs. Harmond wished they could go somewhere else to continue their dispute but they had established the tree as their personal habitat and had no intention of going elsewhere.

Mrs. Harmond sat under the tree and began to hum a hymn to pass time while waiting for her son. She felt hunger dragging relentlessly at her insides. Her small revenue had fallen off because Michannes's parents no longer sent any money and Nickar, Tyrone and Joan-Ann's parents maintained that since the boys' father was in Jamaica, he should take care of them. It was true that the boys were finding help from somewhere but Mrs. Harmond wanted none of what they prepared as she did not know the source. Most of the little she got was spent on medication for Michanne and so there was very little on which to live. Nobody in her family was wealthy and she got the odd dollar infrequently; things were really hard. Leila did what she could and she was the main source, in fact had it not been for her, she could not have afforded Michanne's medication. Mrs. Harmond was not one to bother her children for anything, so she kept silent about her needs and dealt with them when she could. She planned to use the five hundred dollars her son had sent to buy what food supplies she could. She called Jen and sent her to the shop, warning her to be back quickly instead of going off about her business. While she waited, she tried to lock out the birds and keep an eye open for her son. It was almost two-o-clock and he had not turned up yet. He had intimated urgency in his note but must have changed his mind. Maybe what he had found out was not so urgent after all, she tried to reason. Maybe he didn't want to get her hopes up and then smash it to bits with hearsay.

Jen came back two hours later. She claimed the sun was too hot and the shops were packed. Mrs. Harmond knew better but decided not to chide her because the pain in her head was beating a loud, brisk, confusing march. There was a trampling interspersed with light, sharp steps.

She cooked a simple dinner of ground provision and bush cabbage, but she had no appetite so she left hers on the table for later. There was still no sign of Mark even after five-o-clock. She went back to sit under the tree and ignored the miserable birds' disputes. She looked at the distant hills and noted that the white greenery cast by the sun had been replaced by shades of shadow. The sun was on the verge of retiring but lingered a little, leaving a weak, washed out yellow in its wake. As she watched, the brooding hills came alive suddenly when fragments of clouds caught fire, spraying orange flames all over the area. Straggling violet and pink clouds resisted the sprays at first and then merged with them, forming unidentified shapes and a strange hue. Soon they sought release from the huge mass and broke into small puzzle-like shapes and drifted away.

Mrs. Harmond was always fascinated with nature's play of colours at sunset, but this evening she could not give it her full attention as her mind was preoccupied with her son and him not turning up when he had promised he would. She wondered again why he had changed his mind to come and visit her. She didn't want the news he had to give as much as she wanted to see her son, and sit down and talk with him about life and every-thing in general.

She sat on her veranda until eight-o-clock that night. The mosquitos were aboard, they chorused incessantly, directed by their anxiety to get a drop of blood for their supper. Mrs. Harmond tried to cheat them of their meal by slapping at them. Why should they feed on her when she herself had not eaten? She noticed that the moon which had graced the land with its white grin had suddenly been effaced by a scowling cloud. With the moon out of the way, several sombre clouds sailed in and plunged the whole area into blackness. Mrs. Harmond smelt rain and this was sanctioned by the sudden streaks of silver lightning which streamed across the sky, revealing the trees and plants as they undulated in the slight wind which had decided to add its bit to the sudden change in the weather. Even as the lightning played 'now you see me, then you don't', a peal of thunder shook the house. It coincided with fiery, orange lightning which illuminated every crevice of the house and seemed to set the house on fire. A blue light danced on the mirrors and shiny surfaces, and the girls and Jerome started to scream as another ear-splitting peal of thunder rocked the house as though it had a personal vendetta to settle. The girls ran to one another and huddled as if they were experiencing severe cold. They covered their faces and ears in trepidation and crouched as they huddled. They remained like that even after the rain started to beat the roof furiously, creating an incessant sonata of drums.

Mrs. Harmond listened to the rain from her bedroom. She had always loved rain at night as it was soothing and lent itself to lovely dreams. This night it was different, the rain did not palliate her ravelling nerves or help her to lose herself in impossible dreams. Her son had always been a truthful person and she could not understand his failure to turn up when he said he would without sending a message to say he couldn't make it.

The rain ceased after an hour and Mrs. Harmond drifted into an uneasy sleep. At about eleven-o-clock, she was awakened by an awful din in her yard. The dog was barking as if barking would be made illegal at any moment or as if it were going to attract taxes. There was a loud, angry voice shouting at the dog to shut up. Mrs. Harmond knew it was not the boys. She didn't hear them come in but suspected they would be in by then. As she tried to peer through her bedroom window, she heard Nickar's voice.

"A who you out there? Talk fast or leave yah suh! A who you? Talk fast!" He did not call off the dog and when Mrs. Harmond went into the living room, she noticed that he had a long, glistening knife in his hand. She trembled involuntarily and did not go near him. Instead she lit a lantern that was standing on the dining table and held it ready. Almost everyone was awake by now and had come into the living room.

Above the frantic barking, a voice shouted, "Is we Benjy and Clinton. Is we Benjy and Clinton, Grandma is we! Is we Benjy and Clinton!"

Mrs. Harmond moved towards the door holding up the lantern.

"So why you never say that long time!" Nickar shouted, opening the door. He stepped out on the veranda and shouted at the dog, "Yuh ugly mongrel move from roun' yah suh!" When the dog continued to bark, he stepped out into the yard and kicked it. It ran away with a painful yelp.

"Nickar you don't need to kick the dog, all you have to do is run it." Mrs. Harmond was angry at the unnecessary action. She'd had that dog for seven years and it was a marvellous watch dog.

She had noted that Nickar got a frisson from kicking the dog. The pleasure was all too evident in his gleaming eyes, caught in the light of the lantern.

"Come inside, come out of the wet Benjy an' Carlton." Even as she invited them in her heart was doing a hundred metre dash fuelled by fear and worry.

Benjy put down the piece of stick which he had used to defend his brother and himself from the dog and walked into the house. They were hardly inside when Joan-Ann flung the first question at him.

"Is what happen Benjy? Carlton is what happen? If you come down here so late at night after that hard rain is mus' be something. Is Uncle sick or what? Is what?" Her voice held anxiety, over-riding the struggle to keep it calm.

"Joan-Ann be quiet. Don't mention anything like that," Mrs. Harmond remonstrated, looking away from the group crowding the boys. "Benjy, Carlton is what happen? Mi son alright?" She turned to her grandsons with false composure.

"But Mama is the same t'ing me just ask an' you tell me to shut up!" Joan-Ann blurted out, looking at her grandmother as if her mind had gone wandering off.

"Shhh, Joan-Ann don't bother get mama vex," Jerome cautioned in a low voice.

Before Mrs. Harmond could respond, Benjy shouted out like he had a hearing impairment, "Ah really don't know Grandma if something wrong, but ah feel it must be, because from morning papa left the house an' say him a run to town for something an' then run come down here to talk to you bout something important. We don't see him again, so mama sen' us down here to see if him still down here or to fine out what time him come down here an' what time him leave." He said everything in a rush as if something hot was inside his mouth pushing out the words before they burnt him.

"Down here?" Mrs. Harmond said. "Down here! From morning I sitting down here waiting for him an' ah don't see sign of him! Ah was thinking that him change him mind an' would come tomorrow." She paused and looked at her grandsons. "An' then again ah was saying to myself that mi son always keep him word, him is not one to say yeah when him mean nay or the other way around. Him—"

"But this morning when ah was in town in the bus park ah see him an' him say him was coming straight down here," Nickar interjected, quirking his eyebrows.

"Him did leave same time?" Mrs. Harmond asked in a small voice which seemed to be fighting restrain from within.

"Him go an' sit down inside Peter bus what name 'Safe Travel' an' I walk off an' go about my business," Nickar said, his face concealing the concern he had started to feel.

"Lord Jesus him never come down here at all. Ah wait the whole day an' him don't come," Mrs. Harmond repeated, as if she had not said it before. She went and sat at the dining table and stared at the wall as if it could interpret her thoughts and give her the answer. She did not tell them about the note and its contents. If she needed to later, then she would.

The boys left and Mrs. Harmond told them to go straight to the police the next morning if their father did not turn up and then come to inform her about what was happening.

That night she did not sleep at all. She was certain that something was sadly amiss. She took out the note and re-read it several times, hoping that it would present some clues about her son.

Her mind was a maelstrom of possible explanations. She tried to reassure herself that there was a perfectly plausible explanation and that daybreak would herald comforting news. A new day always brought hope that would efface the shadows and uncertainty of night and restore optimism. Despite this reassurance, sleep circumvented her, refusing to come near her eyelids.

She fixed breakfast early, but would not eat a bite of the green bananas and callaloo she had prepared. Her nerves had become unglued and she started at every sound. She got herself ready in case she had to leave the house.

It was a little past six and the sun was just getting used to the idea that its rest was over and it had to start working, when the dog started to bark. Mrs. Harmond rushed outside quickly and sent it away when she saw Tobias, his son, Denzil, Benjy and Carlton and a few other males. She knew right away that her wish for a new day with good news would not be a reality. Tobias came forward and hugged her and she stood still in his arms, her mind an abyss of fear and her limbs a mass of molten bones ready to collapse.

It was Carlton who broke the silence. "Grandma, papa don't come home. We going to the police now." His voice was strained and trembling.

"But why you never go first?" Mrs. Harmond asked, disengaging herself from Tobias who held on tightly to her hand.

"Sister Harry we did go over by Safe Travel to find out where him did come off the bus," Brother Fiddler answered.

"An' what him seh?" Mrs. Harmond asked.

"Him seh Mark come off close to Mr. Heron property," Brother Fiddler supplied.

"Mr. Heron property! That is a good little distance from here. Why him never come off at the usual stop a few chains from here an' then walk down like everybody usually do?" Mrs. Harmond asked incredulously.

"It is just too strange," Brother Fiddler remarked.

"We need to go to the police and then start searching for him," Tobias urged.

They all went to the police station and reported Markdon missing but the police thought it was too early to report him missing. They however consented to get permission from Mr. Heron to search his property since Markdon was last seen in that vicinity.

Mr. Heron resisted at first and wanted to find out what Markdon would be doing on his property when everyone knew that only his workers were allowed there. The police were quick to point out that even though that might be so, he was well aware that trespassing occurred frequently for one reason or another to steal firewood, fruits, ground provisions and even for romantic clandestine meetings. Mr. Heron pretended ignorance even though it was a widely whispered secret that he knew most of what happened on his land and the community in general. He reluctantly agreed but warned that there was to be no destruction of his property or removal of anything that belonged to him.

The police and a large number of volunteers scoured the area but did not find Markdon or anything that could be linked to him. They also searched the adjoining properties and found nothing. One of the properties had what the villagers called a sinkhole and all the searchers stood at a distance and peered into it. They looked fearfully at one another and backed away from it as if it were the entrance to hades. By evening, word had spread over the community and beyond that Markdon had been killed and thrown into the sinkhole. Nobody knew who started the rumour or why, but that was the story that spread like an oil spill on water. The only thing missing from the story was the motive and since they could not come up with one, they all relegated it to the continued generation curse of the family.

No one knew about the note that Mrs. Harmond had shown the police.

The Grandchildren's Activities

Mrs. Harmond was weeding her yam garden. It was slow work because she had passed the age when youth lent her stamina and speed. The weeds were overgrown and stubborn like her grandchildren. She was farming out of necessity but it also gave her something to do, an escape from sitting down suffused with the sorrow that had become her lot. She sang as she tried to defy the noonday sun that wanted to set her body alight. The song, *Swing Low, Sweet Chariot*, was apt in its reminder of the slaves' anguish as they laboured on the plantation. She did not have a slave master with a whip to accelerate her efforts, but the dark memories and the indelible sorrow hung around her, a threat to her sanity and freedom to live like an ordinary human.

She wiped the sweat which raced like tributaries down her face and for a while impeded her vision. She wished that the water was greater and could sweep her away like rapids in a turbulent river. The eddying would wash her mind clean and then she would not have to rue the day she was born.

It was almost a year since Markdon had disappeared and she had received no word from the police or anyone about his disappearance. As some people in the community explained it, wherever he had died, he was under so deep that not even his duppy could escape as no one had even reported ever seeing it. He had not even dreamt to his family.

Mrs. Harmond's thoughts turned to her grandchildren and the events of the past weeks. Most of them were now at the age where they could assert their independence by launching out on a new life of their own, but they remained at Gully Deep and perpetuated their dependence on the family like a baby who could have been walking but was afraid to, and kept holding on to everything it could while tottering around. The only one who showed promise was Jerome. He had passed the required CXC subjects and with his Aunt Leila's help, he was doing further schooling so that he could go away and become an engineer. She was proud of the little light that had beamed its way into her dark path and on the days when despondency deadened her will to live, she was able to fight on. Of course, the disdain he received from the other male relatives made her want to take him away and leave them all behind, but like a rock that was a permanent marker on a landscape, she stayed. Jerome was still afflicted by the strange birthday illness but the effects had become less and less with the passing years.

The other grandchildren were cause for worry. Michanne had good and bad days; some days she would sit by her sister's grave and cry and refuse to talk to anyone except her grandmother. On her good days she would be jovial, laughing and playing around with those around her and even engaging in activities around the house. Joan-Ann, Jen and Simone had become engaged in braiding and combing hair and she would sometimes assist with this. When the girls had commercial activities going on, things were not bad for the family because they would contribute towards buying food. However, business was not always good and on those days there would not be enough to eat, at least for Mrs. Harmond and Jerome.

Melvin, Austin and Elton had got themselves involved in the planting and marketing of ganja. As Mrs. Harmond did her weeding she remembered the surprised shock she got when her suspicions were confirmed. It was early one morning and she had gone into the butchery to search for the hoe which she could not find in the kitchen where she was certain she had placed it.

As she approached the outbuilding a pungent smell wafted its way to her nostrils. She braked suddenly, almost falling forward. She could recognize that smell anywhere; hadn't she lived in the rural area all her life? The real shock was that the smell was coming from a building on her property. She regained her composure and walked purposefully towards the door as if she were going to arrest someone. She angrily wrenched aside the piece of electrical cord that had been used to fasten the door and stepped into the building. Nothing seemed to be out of place but her nose led her to a huge barrel in a far corner. She used to store dried corn, peas and a little peanut but when she opened it, there was nothing of the sort. Instead, dried weed was stacked almost to the top.

"Jesus Christ!" exclaimed Mrs. Harmond, backing away without closing the barrel. "Jesus God. What is this in mi yard?"

"Is what Mama?" asked an irritated voice from the doorway. "What you doing up so early? What you looking for in there?"

She turned around, infuriated. She stepped towards Melvin and swiped at him. He dodged expertly and went back outside in the yard.

"Let me tell you something bwoy, this little piece of bad land belong to me, even though ah don't have no paper with me name on it. My husband, when I did have one, build this piece of butchery an' ah don't remember coming in here an' smelling any nasty illegal weed! How you mean what I doing here, on my own land."

Melvin looked at his grandmother like he was seeing her for the first time. This irate woman spitting anger from pouting lips frightened him. For a while the words cowered in his mouth and then they burst free and escaped. "But Mama you don't hardly come in here. How you jus' get up an' come in here all of a sudden?" There was suspicion in his voice.

"I am very sorry that ah never ask your permission to come into my own place an' that ah never ask you if ah could store weed in your place!" The sarcasm hit Melvin like a bullet but before he could respond, someone else did.

"Mama what you doing in there?" It was Austin, the loud voices had woke both Elton and himself. He had a funny look on his face as if he had been surprised stealing the most expensive jewellery in the world.

"You know what, from now on, ah going to ask your permission to live at this place that has been in this family before my mother's time. But before ah ask you ah going to ask you one thing, tek out you weed out of my butchery before ah do somet'ing evil! Tek it out an' don't bring any more in this yard. An' ah hope that when the police arrest you or when you same criminal fren dem turn against you, you don't look in my direction! Call you mother an' father, is their time now! Call them you hear!"

Austin listened to the voice, it was low at freezing point. It was not the words which his grandmother spoke which caused his heart to freeze in the warm tropical morning. It was the volume and the iciness which clung to his heart. It was the voice of someone who had reached breaking point and was trying to contain emotions teetering on deep resentment and hopelessness. It was the voice of someone who was tired of the every day challenges which came with raising children which were not your own; raising children who had fallen prey to poverty, parental neglect and ignoble deeds. He felt afraid and trembled in the shy morning light but decided to bluff his way out.

"Mama how you expect us to live? We don't have no money or no education an' we not going to beg people roun' here nothing. We have to try for ourself. What you want us to do?"

Austin's plaintive voice bore down upon Mrs. Harmond in the sad morning light. For a moment she struggled with his reasoning, trying to concur with it, but she looked at him defiantly and delivered a verbal blow.

"Bwoy, trouble with the law is not a way out of poverty. Yes you might make some money, but there is three things that come with illegal activity: quick money, quick prison an' quick death! No, crime is not a way out, it better you all go learn a trade since you don't want education. Learn a trade an' take you time an' work your way up in this world. No, weed is not a way out!" She glared at the gathering around her sharply, her eyes filled with deadly knowledge and experience. She looked from one to the other and they were all there except Jen. It was as if she wanted the warning to soak in, for them to absorb it like rain on arid, parched soil in a drought. Not certain that the soil had received it, she sought to saturate their misguided minds with further warning. "Leave illegal activity alone, even if anybody in this world get way with it, you would never get away!" She stopped and studied the faces to see whether her words had fallen on receptive soil or barren, desert land. "Beg you move you weed out of this place as far away from this property as you can. I too old to go to prison!"

She walked away leaving them looking from her to one another. She did not look back but went inside the house and marched into the room where Jen was still sleeping. "Jen wake up right now, ah need to talk to you." Her voice was urgent and no non-sense, but Jen did not stir.

"Jen ah know you hear me so stop pretending! Wake up right now!" She shook Jen roughly and continued to shout. "Wake up right now! Right now, now!" Her voice sounded unfriendly and strained.

"What Mama, is what happen, the house on fire?" Jen sat up reluctantly, pulling the sheet around her and yawning tiredly. Her face looked confused and tense. She kept her face lowered and her eyes averted from her grandmother as if looking directly at her would damage her eyes.

"Little gal ah want you to look straight at me when ah talking to you! Is only people who dishonest an' have something to hide can't look other people in the eye. Which one a them you is?" She peered at Jen angrily, anxious expectancy gleaming in her eyes.

"Mama what happen to you? Why you come wake me out of mi sleep an' a treat mi like criminal?" Jen looked at her grandmother with open irritation and then she looked away and hissed her teeth.

"Jen, little gal don't pass you place! Is who you hissing you teeth at? Is really who you really passing you place with?" Mrs.

Harmond was incensed and highly agitated. She was moving from one foot to the other.

Jen did not answer, she stared steadily at the wall in front of her as if she could see something no one else could.

"Jen tell me something, ah notice that every day after you comb the two little hair you use to go bout your business but of late yuh don't even bother to leave the house an' all you keep doing is sleep an' last night an' the night before you was vomiting!" She paused and looked meaningfully at Jen who kept a steadfast gaze on the wall as if nothing else in the world mattered.

"Jen I have been on this world for more years than ah care to say an' ah know a lot more things than you. One of those things is pregnancy! Jen, little gal why you go get yourself pregnant when you know the situation in this family?" Mrs. Harmond's voice was angry and sad at the same time. Unshed tears were caught in her throat. They throttled in her throat and made her words jerky and unclear.

"Pregnant, who say I pregnant? I never tell anybody that I pregnant." Jen's voice lacked defiance and fire. She didn't sound like Jen, rather like a stranger speaking from Jen's body.

"Jen stop you foolishness, you don't have to tell anybody that you pregnant. It is something that come not go, so me an' everybody else will see in time. You don't have to make any announcement. Jen why you do it? You really don't love youself! Why you creating more problem than this family can bear?" She yanked the sheet from around her and tried to hit her but Jen jumped out of the bed and stood against the wall where she could watch her grandmother's movements. She was like a cornered animal trying to find a small avenue of escape. She twitched her head around like a rabbit or a mouse that was trapped. The tension of the moment was broken by a small, sad voice. "Mama you going to hurt her? Don't lick her, it happen already."

Without looking around Mrs. Harmond knew it was Michanne. Her sadness floated around the room, casting a pall over the room even though the sun was now fully awake.

When Mrs. Harmond finally looked around she saw that everyone was present. Some were directly in the room and the others were hovering in the doorway and in the living room. They had all been drawn by the loud, angry voice of their grandmother. Mrs. Harmond was not necessarily a loud speaker even when she was angry, so they had come quickly to see what was wrong.

Encouraged by Michanne's pleading voice, Jen spoke from her cornered position. "Mama what is really strange about me? As far as I know except for Aunt Leila everybody in this family get pregnant when them young. Can't do better, ah don't have any example to follow. It run in the family, pass down through the generation." For the first time she looked fully at Mrs. Harmond, a look of dogged triumph in her eyes.

To say that Mrs. Harmond was livid was an understatement. She opened her mouth to speak but only choked anger manifested itself in the spluttering words that forced their way out. "You idiot! You big idiot! Even though you don't have much education, even you mus' know that when you inherit a bad situation you try to change it. Instead of trying to get out of this poverty you pushing youself further into it. Tell me, what you doing with baby? Where you going to put it, under the bed or in the butchery? We hardly have space to live as it is much less space for baby! An' ah hope you know who the father is cause this woman not going to raise one more granpickney or any great gran. Ah think ah have paid for my sins on this earth for things ah did when ah was young an' foolish. Cause this life must certainly be a punishment for my deeds! Ah certainly hope you know how you going to find you way out!" She walked off muttering to herself, "Jesus father more shame an' disgrace, where is all this going to end? Lord you sitting up there, tell me what is going to happen to this sick family? Lord ah know yuh know so please tell me!" She threw up her hands in despondency.

As soon as she walked off to sit under the tree, Jen's siblings and relatives gathered around her anxiously.

"Jen, Jesus is how mama fine out so quick? She mus' have a secret pair of eye, Jesus!" Joan-Ann commented in surprise.

"My God man, she really sharp!" exclaimed Simone.

"But you people no real, mama have so much children and live so long why you think she wouldn't fine out?" Nickar interrupted cynically, hissing his teeth and folding his arms.

"But Jen what you really going to do? You tell the baby father?" Joan-Ann was more concerned than inquisitive. "You sure him going to help you with it?"

"No ah don't say anything yet but him is a big man an' him have money so him mus' can deal with him responsibility." Jen spoke assuredly and sat down on the bed, folded her arms and started rocking slowly.

"Jen even though ah don't want to say it but you know mama right. You don't remember what happen to Shanae? You have to be careful of the big man dem cause they only want to play with young girls and then leave them. You better be careful of youself!" Melvin warned, pointing a finger at Jen.

"Ah always think bout Shan an' ah swear is somebody she get mix up with that never into anything serious with her. You better mind youself!" Nickar said. "This family no have no luck for true!"

"Yes Nickar but it happen aready so what ah going to do? Ah not going to be any butcher, something have to work out. An' at the same time Nickar, all you boys better mind yourself, ah sure that you not playing fair yourself. You disappear everyday an' come in late at night. An' then you an' Tyrone knocking head with you father an' his reputation not so good." She looked searchingly at the boys, willing them to dispute her accusation. She was not the only one who had done wrong.

"Jen leave our business alone. We men can take care of ourself!" Tyrone warned. "We cool, we alright, everything roses. Is you girls who need to look out for yourself. Yeah man."

"Jen if I was in your place ah wouldn't tell him yet, wait first. An' you need to tell somebody is who. Shan never tell anybody an' all now we don't even have a suspect to blame." Austin spoke fervently, a troubled look like a sunny day going dark creeping over his face.

"What happen to Shan not going to happen to me cause a going to be careful as of now," Jen said with fierce determination.

"Yes Jen but what Austin say is true, you need to tell somebody is who," Joan-Ann prodded, looking at Jen hopefully.

"Is alright, him say a mustn't tell anybody bout us cause him have a family an' it will cause problem." Jen looked down at the bed and unconsciously twisted her fingers.

"Jesus, Jen, gal you no real! A man tell you that an' you still a continue the relationship? You mad or what? You better try an' don't let mama fine out cause a madness that!" Nickar exploded furiously, looking unbelievably at Jen.

"Alright, alright, how everybody jus' a eat me up so?" Jen responded, flinging out her hands in exasperation and confusion.

"Ah not going back up there right now. Ah going to stay home. Is that alright with all of you?"

"Yes an' when we have anything we will give you, jus' cool an' don't bother answer mama when she talk," Tyrone said soothingly.

Michanne, who was standing by silently all along, suddenly moved away without saying a word. She made her way to Shanae's tomb and sat on it crying for hours, ignoring the pleas of those who were still at home to move away and sit in the house. Mrs. Harmond allowed her to vent her grief and when she thought it was enough, she led her inside and insisted that she eat something, and then she lay on the bed with her until she fell asleep.

One day that same week she went and sat at her favourite place under the tree. The birds were quarrelling furiously. There seemed to be great discontent about the sharing of spoils. Two black birds were fighting over something and were pecking each other mercilessly. Their cries of pain rode the afternoon air and attracted the dog who came running from behind the house, his tail wagging excitedly. He joined in the fracas by barking vehemently as if the spoils belonged to him. Mrs. Harmond, who was already feeling the beginnings of a migraine, was very annoyed at the noise. She flung a stone at the birds, intending only to silence them, and then she chased the dog away. He looked hurt, gave a protesting yelp and slunk away looking back, accusing Mrs. Harmond of disturbing his fun.

No sooner had Mrs. Harmond settled on the bench than she heard, "Miss Harry! Miss Harry where are you?" Mrs. Harmond looked up to heaven. She had looked up to heaven so many times that day that she was afraid her head would get stuck in that beseeching position. She had no pleasure in entertaining Mr. Gustus and with all the problems that day, the prospect of talking to him was daunting. She wished she could just evaporate or sprout wings and fly away.

"Sister Harry, Sister Harry where you are?" The voice was coming closer and closer.

"Roun' here Brother Gustus, you know where ah always is. Ah right here under the tree, where else?" She tried to keep the irritation from her voice.

"Lawd Miss Harry you don't sound too glad to see me but ah had to come. Ah wonder if you know how painful it is to walk come down here? Is only out of the goodness of my heart that ah come, is not to gossip." He limped around the house side and over to the bench where Mrs. Harmond was sitting. His bald head glistened with sweat when he removed his hat. Mrs. Harmond noticed that his face had accumulated more wrinkles and they were grouped up around the cheeks and chin areas like minute tucks in a dress. Mrs. Harmond looked at him and felt a little softening of the heart. "Sit down Brother Gustus, it look like the sun done soak out you strength like sponge."

"You really get it right. A how you keeping Miss Harry? Ah hope keeping good health. You look a little tired but ah can see that you still keeping up." He was asking and answering his own question.

They talked for a while about the happenings in the community: Miss Hemmings' pig that had broken the rope and eaten down Zakariah's peanut and how he had gone into Miss Hemmings' yard and stoned the pig to death. Mr. Jennings' daughter was only twenty but had delivered her fourth baby, a little boy that looked like john crow was baking bread to eat him; and Mr. Eaton's fifteen year old daughter who had been diagnosed with a strange illness and had been hospitalized, and the prognosis was bleak as the doctor said it was only a matter of time before she answered to her number.

Mrs. Harmond knew that Mr. Gustus had not only come to discuss other people's business but would soon get around to some matter relating to her family. She participated in the conversation with half of her senses speculating on the real reason for his visit. He finally got around to it.

"Miss Harry where the boys dem?" He lowered his voice and looked towards the house as if he expected them to come through the front door or appear at the side of the house.

"Your guess is as good as mine, the only one that ah have a good idea about is Jerome since him gone to school." Mrs. Harmond's heart quickened to racing proportions, she was quite certain that Mr. Gustus could hear it reverberating.

"Them not here then, good. The argument stink all over the community that three a your grandson involve in the ganja business." He looked at Mrs. Harmond to see the effect of the announcement and was a little disappointed that her face was expressionless, as dead as if he had told her that night would follow day. "Yes, them involve an' strange man dem coming to them when it dust to buy weed. Dem an' Miss Ermine an' Mr. Hayle boy dem from up the community. Mi hear say dem into it big. Mi hear that two nights ago, man with big van was at the top of the hill a buy weed from them. Ah come to warn you to make sure that is not close to you house them storing it cause if police search the place an' fine it, you gone too!" His voice had become even lower but there was a deathly warning in the lowered tones. "Ah know you for too long to sit back an' don't warn you, cause you know that everything is a big talking in this place an' very soon it going to reach the police ears. Moreover them ganja thing deh never always go right an' sometimes big fuss an' quarrel come out of it an' cause injury an' death." He delivered his last piece of warning and then became silent.

The only sounds that could be heard were the tapping of his stick and the sound of the birds who had started their feud again. Mrs. Harmond remained silent, it would appear as if she did not understand Mr. Gustus because she just sat like a piece of steel buried in the ground.

"Sister Harry, you understand what me just say to you?" Without waiting for an answer, he continued, "Make certain that you check you premises an' you better tell the boy dem to leave here so for a while cause too much people a talk."

After he hobbled away, Mrs. Harmond continued to sit under the tree. Somehow she knew it would have come to this, it was only a matter of time. When she had found out for certain about the boys' activity she had spoken to them repeatedly but to no avail. It was not strange for young men in the community to deal in drug activities, sometimes there were even females helping them to package weed for sale. Some of them used the money to take care of their families and build houses. There were whispers of so-called influential people who were involved. It was said that the poorer young men worked for them, planting and reaping and that the big players would find the market and then share the proceeds with them. The trouble with this was that the ones lower down were the ones who got into trouble. Police raided their property and they would be locked up, or there would be disagreements and fights. The worse part of the scenario was that other crimes arose from this activity, other drug use, guns, death over spoils not properly shared, etc.

Mrs. Harmond knew that nothing good would come out of it for her grandsons. She preferred to endure hardships rather than knowingly partake of earnings from that source. She was always pejorative about their behaviour and this had driven wedges into their relationship. The close, filial ties that once existed were loosening and her grand-children often avoided her, fearing reprimand for their behaviour. Jerome and Michanne were the two most respectful ones. She was beginning to feel like an alien among them but she was not prepared to just sit idly by and not say anything. It should never be said that she had not tried. She would talk to them again, that was the least she could do. She knew that when one person in the family was in trouble, the whole family was in trouble.

She seized the opportunity to talk to them the following morning when they were preparing to leave. She didn't want to quarrel with them, just talk.

"Boys ah want you to listen to me a little before you leave," she started lamely.

"Lawd have mercy a what now?" Melvin looked at his grand-mother and his demeanour changed from nonchalant to defensive.

"Boys, word is out that you mix up in selling ganja an' even though ah talk to you just a few days ago ah talking again." She did not know what to do but to attack the problem head-on.

"But Mama, you done talk already and we done tell you how the t'ing set." Melvin looked at his grandmother as if she had be-come senile and was in need of pity.

Mrs. Harmond was not deceived and saw the look, but she continued. "I do not want to see anything bad happen to any of you. I am not your enemy, I am your friend. You are young an' have the whole of your life in front of you, don't spoil it getting into the easy way of life, don't—"

"Mama, nothing no easy about slaving in the sun whole day, not a single t'ing an' you know how that go." Melvin was not giv-ing up his defence of the way he had chosen to go.

"Yes that may be so but you slaving at the wrong thing! Ah begging you to try an' go learn a trade an' leave this weed thing alone. Ah don't know what you two go away an' do every day but ah begging an' pleading to you to be careful what you do. Ah tired of the problems in this family. Too much hurt an' death. We have to do something to help ourself an' to stop the destruction."

"Well Mama what must happen must happen, you an' me can't stop it!" Elton's voice held determination; his grandmother was not going to be the one to change his mind. "Well Mama right now ah going down the river to tek a swim and wash off some a the crosses people in this place out a my mind. Forget bout dem Mama, just like how when ah hit the water ah won't member anything about dem. An' ah going to carry back some fish for you to." He added the last in an attempt to stop her from saying anything else about the sore topic.

"Well before you go ah hope you take out everything out of the butchery. As ah said before I too old to go to prison." She did not know how else to plead. She stood aside and watched them go.

Two weeks later, plagued by a migraine which had become a part of daily life, Mrs. Harmond went to her bed as soon as it became dark, leaving the girls awake. Jerome was working on an assignment that was due later that week.

She awoke about one-o-clock to the sounds of excited talking coming from the hall. She got up and went into the hall to find out why they were not asleep at that time of the morning and had insisted on waking her up.

"What is all this noise for? Why you all not sleeping? Morning come already!" She looked from one face to the other and noticed that the faces were glum. "What is the problem? Why you all look like somebody sick or dead?" Even as she asked an unknown feeling started from her toes, weakening her knees like a frail weed being blown by a heavy wind. It moved up to her stomach and spread all over like warm melted butter. It tugged at her heart and protesting at the disturbance, her heart stepped up its normal rate of operation. The pain in her head gave way to an unsteadying weakness that threatened to liquefy the contents in her brain. Inwardly, she struggled against the surge and asked the question again. "Why you not sleeping an' why you face look like that?"

The group started laughing then Tyrone said, "Is alright Mama, everything alright. We just a little concerned cause Austin and Elton don't come home yet an' we trying to call them but them not answering. It look like them gone to late movie in town." The group laughed again and Mrs. Harmond wondered at their whimsical behaviour. She wondered if they were trying to appease her; first they looked sad, afterwards a bit happy.

"Do they normally go to town to watch movie this late?" Mrs. Harmond wanted to know.

"Ah think they might be watching a double," Jen explained. "Some new shows come down since last week."

Mrs. Harmond went back to lie down but she could not sleep. She could hear the dog barking fiercely as if it were directly attacking someone. Soon it gave a yelp and the barking petered off. There was a knock at the door and Mrs. Harmond breathed a sigh of relief, most certainly that must be the boys. She listened as someone opened the door.

"Boy you tek it late tonight eh. So where is Elton, what him doing outside?"

"Elton! Elton not outside, him not with me. Him leave from ten-o-clock say him going to talk to somebody an' then come straight home. Him come an' leave again?" Austin's voice held surprise.

"Come! Him don't come back here since him leave from morning. Ah thought him was with you!" The gruff voice sounded like Nickar's.

"Well him soon come then cause it well late now. The movie was too wicked for me to leave before it done an' then when it done ah couldn't get no drive, that's why ah coming back so late," Austin explained.

"Well it not late anymore, is early morning now. You know you take a chance walking when the dog 'fraid especially when you just collect money." The lowered voice belonged to Tyrone.

Mrs. Harmond was just able to make out the response. "Nobody an' ah mean nobody can't find my money where I hide it an' even if them hold me up me ah still not telling them where to fine it. Check out this reasoning, if you tell them, them going to kill you an' if you don't tell them, them still going to kill you so I prefer to die an' deprive them, a jus' so the t'ing set." Austin sounded as if he had his life well-reasoned out.

Two-o-clock came and went and so did three, four, five and six-o-clock and Elton had not turned up. The pain in Mrs. Harmond's head was now a circuit of pain; first her forehead, then the left side of her head, then the right, then the back. She had been sitting motionless since she had awakened out of a fitful sleep at four-o-clock. She started to hum a song to herself but it sounded hollow and insincere. She stopped, cleared her throat and started it again, but soon abandoned it for a low, monotone hum which sounded like a machine with a broken spring.

The boys formed two groups; one group went into the community to make enquires, while another group went into the bushes where Mrs. Harmond figured the ganja cultivation was done. She could not concentrate on household chores and neither could she eat so she went and sat on the bench under the tree. The girls followed her silently like shadows compelled to accompany the corporeal form. Michanne sat beside her and placed her head in her lap. Mrs. Harmond placed one hand around her and stroked her head like she would a little girl. As Mrs. Harmond settled down, she realized that something was wrong, but she could not identify what it was.

After a minute or two it hit her forcefully, how could she not have realized it when the silence bellowed at her. The birds were quiet. There was not a single sound coming from the tree. No fiery disputes, no loud squawking, no drilling of wood and frivolous chattering. Mrs. Harmond was perplexed. Could they have migrated? She was happy for the silence but it was really uncanny. She never thought she would miss those annoying birds.

They sat there for about two hours awaiting the boys' return. There was very little talking. Words seemed to have taken a vacation just like the birds. Michanne was fast asleep in Mrs. Harmond's lap, lulled to sleep by the comforting head rub.

News, especially bad, always zoomed around the community like an orbiting rocket by some neighbours from over the hill and sure enough, other family members showed up. Tobias, Leila, her husband and Laurine and others whom Mrs. Harmond had not seen since Markdon's disappearance. They had only heard that Elton could not be found and knowing what had been happening in the family, they had all gathered expecting the worse and at the same time expecting a miracle. They all made jokes about Elton going off with a girl, or going off to do private business or stealing off to shop with some of his new earnings. The jokes lacked real mirth and the laughter was only at face level.

The first group to come back was the one which had gone

into the bushes. The boys did not have good news. The little hut the boys had built in the bushes had been knocked to pieces and some ganja which had been stored in it had disappeared. Somebody had also destroyed an area where some young plants had been growing. This information was given very softly and soberly. Mrs. Harmond hoped it would not be reported to the police even though the information would help them in their conjecture about what had happened if Elton did not turn up.

About an hour later, the second group came back with the news that they had not seen or heard anything about Elton. They had gone into town where he was last seen and questioned some people whom they had seen at the movie, but no one had any information. A group of people left to report Elton's disappearance to the police while others sat with Mrs. Harmond and waited.

Soon after the group left, Who Dat and another young man tore down the hill as if blood hounds were chasing them. The urgency of the feet told everyone present that it was all over, the mock-fun, the subversion of pessimism, the false hope were all gone as Who Dat burst into the yard. He was wearing an old straw hat patched with pieces of coloured fabric where the straw had given way, two old pants, one long and torn and the other short and frayed at the legs. The old, fish net merino completed his fatuous appearance but no one took the time out to point and laugh at him. He steamed into the yard and could not stop at the bench where Mrs. Harmond was sitting because of his great speed. He reminded Leila of a ship that had run aground. When he finally got his balance, he did a pirouette and then stepped over to Mrs. Harmond and the others who were waiting in anguish for him to speak.

"Who Dat why the devil you don't stop you antics and settle down!" Mr. Gustus shook his stick at him threateningly.

"Brother Gustus stop you violence in this serious time. Miss

132

Harry, O God Miss Harry, death multiply an' minus in your family!"
He put his hands on his head, pressing down the ridiculous hat
and then setting it askew on his head.

"Idiot talk fast or jus' shut up!" Tobias walked towards him,
palms open.

"Maas Toby calm down, calm down sah an' listen. Ah went
down a river to draw mi fish pot an' ah see something a float on
the water. Mi run cause mi 'fraid an' mi call out to some man
nearby. Them come an' then dem go into the water. Ah don't
follow them cause mark you mi 'fraid. Dem take out a body an'
when mi listen dem bawl out say a Elton. Jesus Christ, Elton
drown!" He spun and held his head and folded and unfolded his
arms.

The howling and screaming which followed could only be
described as horrific. It was like a menagerie which had somehow
been disturbed and the animals were protesting in any way that
they could.

Mrs. Harmond, matriarch and burden bearer, sat frozen like
a bold exclamation mark. Her body had lost its capacity to react,
all her faculties had collapsed. The tear ducts had refused to be
productive, her thought process had been eclipsed, and inertia
had set in. Once more the disease – death – had struck her family
in a virulent manner. It seemed to be the order of her life; it was
only a matter of who was next in line.

That day the community council gathered once more to do
its post mortem of the event. They gathered along the shop piazza
and road side and stooped, sat and stood, all anxious to give their
comments. The tide had changed somewhat and the usual censure
ascribed to the family curse waned a little. "Oh God it get too
much now!" Green Lizard declared. "Too much! Why everything

just a happen to one set a people so? Ah mean other young bwoy bout the place involve in a the weed thing and nobody don't even notice them much less so what is the big thing?" His voice held shock and deep regret.

"Ah mean yes we have other people dying in the community but is from ordinary sickness. Lawd man them never have to do the bwoy so, kill him an' then throw him in the river! A born wickedness dat!" The man sitting on the stool was trembling. His visage clearly showed the deep sympathy he felt.

"Mi just feel that is one and the same people that him do business with! Somebody must know something! Something must come out of this one. The youth no deserve fi dead so just because him make a little money. The family well poor an' it would help them a little even though you see that Miss Harry she no really mix up in them kind a t'ing!"

"Boy something other than the curse really wrong an' a think is time people start look for some answer. High, high time!" The speaker looked around at his audience for support and saw faces which registered questions, uncertainty and mystified looks.

Further Happenings

It was five months after Elton's funeral and Mrs. Harmond was hanging out some clothes on the line. As usual, she tried to sing. It was a very good way to remind herself that there was a God even though there were some who believed that He had abandoned her family and that her going to church was an exercise in futility. A few sceptics shared the opinion that the sins of the family were so grave that not even God wanted to have anything to do with them. Just look at how he was killing them one by one despite Mrs. Harmond's love for church.

Mrs. Harmond's faith was nearly shaken. She knew all the things that people were saying because her grandchildren openly discussed everything they heard. She also knew that there were a few people who were having second thoughts about the so-called curse. She braved the comments and still went to church, listened to the messages, ignored the jabs and paid attention to what applied to her as a person. Her spirit was in the pits and the space in her heart widened every day. She doubted that anything would ever fill it again. Her feelings were too deep, too intense, too much like a cavern which held deep secrets, thoughts and half clues and ideas which she kept subverted. Most people were of the opinion that she was headed for a psychotic breakdown because she had not cried in all her misfortune. How could one woman bear so much and not shed tears when even males had done so?

She heard a sound close to the back of the house and looked around. It was Austin, or rather Austin's shadow. Mrs. Harmond watched as the slim, young man placed a pair of sneakers on a boulder and then stood staring at nothing in particular. She noted again his deep, sunken eyes which looked like raisins in a dark fruit cake. His face had been robbed of its ruddy, youthful look and the hardened, aged face of a man who had borne anguish stared back at you. It was fashionable for some males to drop their pants on the brink of their bottoms but Austin's pants had fallen there naturally because he had lost so much weight. His pants were like a wide, gathered skirt. He ate only enough to keep the wind from blowing him away and spent most of his time just lying on the veranda staring out into the atmosphere. As far as Mrs. Harmond knew, he had given up his illegal economic activity. He no longer got up and went anywhere, not even to town. He had received much censure from the community about doing business with total strangers. It was their opinion that one of them had killed Elton.

Mrs. Harmond turned back to her activity when Austin went back inside. Her mind turned to his parents. They had not attended the funeral at all, but had sent money to offset the expenses. The consensus was that since they had contributed so little to their children's welfare, they feared that they would receive the same treatment as Shanae's parents. The whole community criticized them, marvelling at the fact that Mrs. Harmond's grandchildren had been completely abandoned into her care. This was true as she only received the occasional few pounds from her children. Joan-Ann sometimes received a little money from her brothers but Mrs. Harmond encouraged her not to take anything from them because she did not know what they and their sneaky, good for nothing father were up to. She was sure they were up to no good but she told herself that whatever was to be, had to be. What could she do about it when she talked and talked and nobody but Jerome listened?

She hurriedly hung the clothes on the line because she wanted to accompany Jen to the hospital for her medical check up. She was past seven months now and had to go in every two weeks. She had decided at first not to have anything to do with her and her pregnancy, but she could not find it in her heart to ignore her, especially after she had learnt some interesting and important information.

It was two months before and she was lying in bed trying to sleep. The girls apparently thought she was asleep and so they openly discussed Jen's situation.

"Jen what the man say about the baby? You getting money from him?" Joan-Ann's voice held curiosity and interest.

For a long while there was no answer. Mrs. Harmond strained her ears to hear the response but Jen said nothing.

"Jen all of us live here so for years now an' if you have a problem we need to know. Who else you think will help you if you have a problem?" Simone sounded concerned and eager.

"Yes Jen you need to tell us what going on. We know that Nickar an' Tyrone helping you out, but what bout the father?" Michanne's voice sounded sad.

"Well," Jen began. She sounded vague and reluctant. "The baby father don't really want to have nothing to do with any baby. Him say him is not the father an' if a call him name an' cause any problem in him life it not going to be nice." Her voice petered off sadly and there was a suggestion of tears in it.

Mrs. Harmond was somehow not shocked at what she was hearing. For some reason she felt that if Shanae had confided in anyone the two stories would have been similar. She felt that both girls had got themselves involved with men who were not really interested in them as persons. They probably ignored the young men who lived in the area because they were poor and didn't have any money to offer them. The girls probably thought these adults could help them financially but it would have been better for them if they had settled for love instead. She dragged herself from her reverie when Simone broke the thunderous silence that had followed Jen's comment.

"But Jen is who? You need to tell us is who! You need to tell even mama so that she can go an' talk to him bout giving you something for the baby!" Simone sounded frantic.

"You mad! Ah don't want mama to know anything at all bout this business!" Jen lowered her voice urgently. "As a matter of fact you certain she sleeping? You better go an' look," she said in a loud whisper.

Mrs. Harmond could feel the eyes boring into her and she laid as still as a stone. She even added slight snoring to make it more authentic.

"She dead to the world," Joan-Ann reported. She then added, "Jen you see because of what happen to Shan an' all the wicked things that keep happening to the family, ah think we shouldn't hide these things from mama. She is practically our mother an' in spite of all the problems ah think she still love us."

Michanne's melancholy voice chipped in. "You know ah feel that even if you don't tell her, she know that something wrong. Ah feel sometimes that mama know some things that she not telling anybody. Ah feel she know some secrets or have a good idea about some things that for some reason she keep to herself."

For a moment Michanne sounded like an old, experienced person. Even though some people felt that her brain had power outages sometimes, her reasoning sometimes shocked Mrs. Harmond. She cringed where she laid, wondering what had led Michanne to that conclusion. Her ears pricked up like a hound following a scent when she heard Jen's response.

"Mama talk little bit an' she listen a lot. Ah always get the feeling that she know something bout Shan that she never tell anybody. But ah still don't want to tell her bout this problem. Ah going to keep pretending that everything alright for her sake an' mine. Ah..." Jen's voice trailed off into an uncomfortable silence.

"Jen you better make certain that you don't go back anywhere near that man. Make certain that you always go out with some-body an' when you have the baby you better give it your surname. Even though you can prove to the man dat is his child, one, you don't have the money for them fancy DNA an' two, you don't want to have any problem with no man an' him woman or wife. Ah just get the impression that is a married man." Joan-Ann's voice was coaxing, persuasive. She was trying to get a little information out of Jen.

"Joan-Ann just leave it alone." Jen sounded a little scared and worried. "Even if ah tell you a name you still not going to know him, an' ah don't want anybody in this family walking around an' asking anybody any question."

"Jen ah think that when you have the baby, you should go to the country for a while. Ah just have a bad feeling that there

might be some trouble an' ah don't think this family can take anything else." Michanne's voice choked on her tears.

"Michanne please, don't bother cry. Please Michanne, everything going to be all right. Don't get upset. Ah don't mean to
cause any trouble an' make you feel sick. Hug me up." Jen went
over to her and hugged her.

Mrs. Harmond heard sniffing and then there was silence; the
girls had moved away. Some of Mrs. Harmond's worst fears had
been confirmed. The thought that lightning did not strike in
the same place twice was a myth. What was true was that it did
not always strike in the same way. Like Shanae, Jen was having
a similar problem – getting involved with the wrong man and
being abandoned. These children did not listen or learn from
all the misfortune of the family. They would simply have to learn
the hard way. She had done all she could to guide them but sometimes it seemed they were beyond guidance; only God could help
them.

After hanging up the clothes she had breakfast, got ready and
accompanied Jen to the hospital. She kept very close to her on
the bus and while she was walking to the maternity section of
the hospital, she did not know what to expect and she did not
feel that she should leave her alone again until she had the baby
and they could come up with a plan with what to do with her.
Michanne's suggestion of sending her to the country was a good
one, but she would not say anything to her yet, she did not want
the news to leak.

While Jen was being attended to in the clinic, Mrs. Harmond
felt thirsty and went to drink some water. She'd had her last
two children at the hospital and she knew her way around very
well. She went to the water cooler on the delivery ward. There

were two long benches in front of the ward and family members, spouses and friends were anxiously awaiting news of the birth of their loved ones' babies or waiting to take their loved ones home. On her way back to Jen's section, Mrs. Harmond bumped into a man who was standing at the end of one of the benches rather than sitting on it.

"Sorry Sir, so sorry," Mrs. Harmond said apologetically.

The man did not answer and Mrs. Harmond looked up at him. She stepped back in surprise. "You, what you doing here?" It was Rita's husband Pete, and he was not happy to see her. His face was a mixture of pain, embarrassment and hate. Mrs. Harmond felt anger surging in her like oats ready to boil over the edge of the pot.

"Old woman, move out a mi way." He spoke through clenched teeth as if his teeth were pasted together.

"At least I live to see old age but you won't get that privilege. Shame an' embarrassment going to kill you cause the baby dead again, ah can see it in your face!" It was the first time that Mrs. Harmond was speaking to him since Rita's death. All the pent up hurt and anger released itself like a dormant volcano that had been threatening to erupt for years. "What you going to do with the woman now, kill her like how you kill Rita?"

Pete opened his mouth in shock and then he gave Mrs. Harmond a hideous look which would have killed her instantly if looks could kill. "What you talking bout old woman? I never tell Rita to kill herself!" He was whispering loudly, trying not to attract the attention of the people nearby.

"Rita would never kill herself, the doctor said she took a whole heap of sleeping pills an' I know Rita, you have problem getting her to take one pill much less so much. From Rita was a child she couldn't swallow pill, we had to dissolve it in water. Even when she go to hospital they have to empty out all the capsule. Rita never have no sleeping pill, nowhere to take! When you bring the water go give Jen the night when Rita dead, you dissolve the pill them in the water an' give Jen to give her! You murder her cause the baby dem dead! You is a wicked, murderous wretch!" Mrs. Harmond's whole body was shaking, she feared she would fall over or burst a blood vessel.

Pete looked at Mrs. Harmond with his eyes and mouth opened as if he had seen Rita's ghost standing by her mother's side. His first attempt at speech failed and he eyed her with a satanic glare. "Old woman you can't prove none of you rubbish! You can't prove nothing bad bout me! You a idiot and ah going fix your business if you call up mi name to anybody!" He moved threateningly towards her.

Mrs. Harmond did not move. "Even if you hit me it not going to change anything you did or anything ah just said. An' what you going to do now that your girlfriend baby dead too? You going to kill her like you kill Rita?" Her eyes were small sharp daggers that stabbed at Pete.

He raised his hands and lowered them, then quickly raised his right hand and before he could change his mind, he hit her once across the face, a resounding slap that sent her head revolving a full ninety degrees. She staggered backwards and slumped against the wall, and then down abruptly on the floor. Pete took one look at Mrs. Harmond and ran off. The security guard didn't quite know what had happened but he saw a woman sinking to the ground like a heavy piece of wood falling and a man with fright leaping out of his eyes taking off, so he started to chase him.

Pete was sleight of foot and the security guard had a hard time following him. In addition, he seemed to know the hospital grounds very well and he dodged around a building close to the road and escaped through an aperture in the fence, into the nearby community. The security guard was annoyed at what he regarded as his clumsiness but walked back quickly to his station and found a small gathering around the fallen woman.

"Excuse me, excuse me, hot water trolley coming through!" he called out loudly as he bulldozed his way through the gathering.

"Instead of gathering roun' the lady an' trying to stifle her, why somebody no call one of the nurse?" the security guard asked in a surprised and annoying tone.

"But we call her already an' she say she busy an' she gone to call someone else," a lady that was bending over Mrs. Harmond volunteered.

"But look how long she gone, suppose a dead the woman dead!" The incensed bystander looked over her shoulder at the doorway through which the nurse had gone.

"Nurse! Nurse! Somebody sick bad out here!" an elderly lady rushed in slow time to the door and shouted.

"Is so some of these nurses stay, is like you have to beg them to give quick attention sometimes," another lady posited her opinion.

"Yes that's how we are sometimes because around here there is just too much to do and only a few nurses to do it. If you take careful notice you will see that the nurses, like yourself, have only two hands. They are not from outer space where those creatures have extra limbs!" The nurse came towards them talking as she approached the small crowd. The crowd parted and allowed her through and she took charge. "Security, please call one of the porter, tell him to bring a stretcher for the patient. And in the meantime could you kindly move aside so she can get some air. Also who is she here with?"

Everyone looked around at the next person and then one elderly lady said, "She was sitting over here with us, ah think she was coming from the cooler."

"Did anybody see what happened?" the nurse enquired, looking around at the faces.

"She was talking to a man an' him box her an' run an' she drop."

At the same time the porter came and the security guard helped him to place Mrs. Harmond on the stretcher.

"Let me know if anyone comes asking for her," the nurse said, following the stretcher.

As soon as Mrs. Harmond was wheeled in, Pete's girlfriend came out. She could hardly walk, her feet were as swollen as inflated balloons and her long face looked tired and dejected as befitted one who had just gone through a gut wrenching ordeal and was happy to be alive. Her face had long, meandering lines of dried tears. The bag she had in her hand seemed too heavy and was about to fall.

The security guard came to her rescue. "Mummy give me the bag and sit down before you fall down." He helped her to a nearby vacant seat. "Who come to meet you?" Cathy sat down gratefully and looked around.

"Pete is supposed to be out here but ah don't see him. Him come long time an' call to me but ah don't see him now." She sounded sad and disappointed, assuming that he had left because he had nothing with which to prove his manhood to his community.

The woman who had given the nurse the information about the incident said, "Miss, describe him."

"Him tall an' black an' him have some bump in him forehead. Him was wearing a jeans pants an' a black tee shirt an'—"

"Is the same evil wretch that box down the old woman an' run gone," said a woman seated opposite to her. "The same ugly wretch! Miss a so him beat you?"

"Beat who? Beat who? Him don't even talk that much. The woman must do him something why him hit her." Her defence of Pete was lame and untrue because recently he had become silently aggressive and frequently looked at her as though he wanted to beat her up when she complained about anything.

"Excuse me, anybody see an elderly lady, short, small, brown with some black spots on her face?" It was Jen, her examination was finished and she was searching for her grandmother whom she had expected to be seated outside her area but was not there.

"That sound like the lady the man lick down," a woman seated in the group answered. "She inside the hospital, the nurse dem looking after her," she further supplied in a loud voice as if Jen was deaf. "Who is she? It must be your grandmother."

Jen eyes filled up with tears, she enquired, "What you mean a man lick her down? My grandmother don't normally trouble people so how come this man lick her? Him must mistake her for somebody else!" Her voice was incredulous, shocked. "Can you describe the man Miss?" Jen looked at the woman expectantly.

"Ah think that woman over there is the best person to ask that." The speaker pointed towards Cathy. "Maybe you know her, is her man."

Jen followed the finger and sneered insolently at Cathy. "Pete! Pete! You mean Pete lick my grandmother! My grandmother is the one who should lick him! You need to tell me why Pete hit my grandmother." She started wobbling over to Cathy like a bug pushing a heavy load in front of it. A look of hate kindled in her eyes.

145

"Miss, Miss, you better sit down before you deliver before time! Mine you hurt yourself cause you can't fight nobody with that big belly." The first lady who had spoken got up and walked over towards her and guided her reluctantly towards a seat. At the same time Cathy got up and walked away, disbelief and embarrassment carved in her face.

As Jen sat down, she struggled awkwardly up again. "Ah need to see what is happening to mama. Ah need to know if she going to be alright." She started ambling towards the door but stopped in her tracks when she saw her grandmother and a nurse coming towards her. The nurse held Mrs. Harmond's hand and guided her to a seat.

"Mama you alright?" Jen inquired with concern. "Mama what happen, how this happen?"

"Yes Jen, ah jus' get knock out for a time. Ah will be alright soon as ah get some more rest, just a little more rest." She did not answer Jen's second question. She closed her eyes and rested her head on the wall. Her face looked older, drawn and thin as though her life blood was leaking to an unknown source.

Jen looked at her grandmother and new, immediate knowledge of her suffering dawned upon her. She wondered just how much more she would be able to bear. Why didn't God help her? Her grandmother had been faithful, not neglecting her church for long even when things were at their worst. Sudden fear grabbed her at the thought of something serious happening to her. She knew that the whole family would crumble like a water-soaked cookie. She was the nucleus, the brain, the hub of their world, the only real mother that they knew. She made a secret pledge to pay more attention to her admonitions and her well-being. She struggled to her feet and begged the woman who was sitting beside her grandmother to allow her to sit next to her. She could not hug her because of her huge stomach, so she held her hand tightly as if she was afraid of letting go and getting lost.

The loud screaming of the ambulance invaded her thoughts and she looked towards the hospital gate and saw the ambulance flashing through as though it was involved in motor racing.

"Bwoy, I going down to see what going on," one woman announced inquisitively.

"Me too," said another, getting up hurriedly.

"But ah don't understand you woman. Don't this is a hospital and the ambulance come in all the time, who you expect to be in it but sick people?" This came from the woman sitting next to Jen.

The two women walked away without responding. From where she was, Jen watched as a small crowd went towards the ambulance and then later saw a security guard speaking to them agitatedly. The crowd parted and the paramedics came out with a stretcher between them and rushed into the emergency building.

Jen turned her attention back to her grandmother. Her eyes were still closed and she wondered if she was asleep. "Mama you alright? Ah going to call a taxi so we can get home quick. The bus usually pack up and take too long."

While she was talking on the phone, the two women who had gone to see what was happening by the ambulance came rushing back quickly. They were excited.

"Why you two look so excited, is what? Somebody kill Satan an' set us free?" It was the same woman who had criticised them earlier. Everybody started to laugh.

"You can always laugh an' call us inquisitive but wait till you hear this. Guess who dem jus' take them out of the ambulance? Guess who?" She was in a boxing ring, all she needed were boxing gloves and boxing attire, the opponent was already down. "Wooi, this one is a sample!"

"My girl, stop the gymnastic and talk. Better yet, let me ask the other woman that did go with you. Miss, is who was in the ambulance?" The voice bordered on impatience and irritability.

Not wanting to have her thunder stolen from her, the reporter cried out, "Wait nuh, wait, is me telling the story! Since you can't guess is who let me tell you. Wooi father, is the same man that clout the lady over there so the big box!"

"Jesus Christ what you mean the same man!" Another lady stood up, incredulous; she could not contain herself.

"My girl the same man that box the woman. My girl the ambulance driver say nothing more than him a stranger in the community and somebody shoot him say him a spy from cross the next side!" She threw up her hands and pranced around some more.

"Him dead or what?" asked another woman.

"It no look so but it don't look like him going to live."

"This is not reaction, this a quick action," another lady commented in awe. "Him jump out a frying pan an' jump right in a fire. Ah really don't know him but if a so him treat old people then him can't be a good man!"

Mrs. Harmond and Jen sat stunned as if they were in a stupor. What the lady was reporting could certainly not be true, but the other woman had not denied it and she could see no reason for her inventing such a story.

Later that evening after they got home, Mr. Gustus doddered over to tell the story. He had heard that Pete had succumbed to his injuries. Mrs. Harmond did not disclose anything about the hospital incident to him. She just listened without comment. She knew that soon the community would hear because Pete's girlfriend would most certainly tell them a part of what had transpired. Only her family members knew the reason for her attack because she had at last revealed the real reason for Rita's mysterious death.

E E E

Mrs. Harmond was again at the hospital, accompanied by Michanne and Joan-Ann. Jen had been admitted two days before in excruciating pain and the doctor had said he would have to do a caesarean section if she had not delivered the night before. Even though she had been averse to the whole idea of Jen's pregnancy, she was looking forward to seeing the baby. Maybe new blood, a new generation, would inject some luck into the family and tempt fate to reverse the so-called curse that was killing off the members of her family.

While going through the hospital gate she noticed several people going out with babies; there were happy couples and those with mixed expressions on their faces. There were also single mothers struggling with their newborn and the babies' bags. There was even a man alone with a baby. He was wearing a grey hooded jacket and the hood was partially over his bent head. He seemed to be studying the features of his newborn. Mrs. Harmond chuckled inwardly at the idea that some men were sometimes thrilled if the baby bore a resemblance to them, that way they were sure that it was their offspring. She wondered about the mother. Where was she?

They were early for visiting hours so they sat outside and waited with the other visitors. Joan-Ann had a camera ready to take the baby's picture. She even had a list of possible names that she wanted Jen to consider. She hoped it would be a little girl.

She figured that it would be much more fun caring for a baby girl. Mrs. Harmond had told Jen that she should register the baby in her surname as she did not want to disclose the father's name and more over he did not seem interested. As far as she knew he had not given her a cent towards the baby.

She rushed in with the girls when the visiting time came to find Jen half asleep. She looked worn-out and tired as if she had been on a long, arduous journey and was trying to recover. Mrs. Harmond's heart went out to her and she hoped that the experience would deter her from engaging in adult behaviour.

"Wake up Mummy," Joan-Ann joked as she approached Jen's bed. "You are a mother now so you can't sleep off an' leave the baby alone." She reached over and hugged her.

Jen struggled awake and sat up unsteadily. "An' of course you come with excitement. Let me ask the nurse to bring her in. Boy she really pretty. Wait till you see her!" She smiled weakly but the excitement and pride were evident in her eyes. "Nurse," she called to a nurse who was walking past her bed. "Nurse can you bring the baby for me? My family is here to see her."

The nurse nodded and went off. All around her family members were either coming in or had already surrounded the beds of their families and friends. They were admiring the newborn babies and laughing. Mrs. Harmond knew from experience that all was not necessarily well with the mothers but for the moment all the problems seemed to be forgotten.

They waited about five minutes and the nurse did not return. The nursery was just next door so they wondered what was taking her so long.

"Maybe the baby mess up an' she changing him," Michanne offered, looking impatiently in the direction of the nursery.

"Ah going to find out what keeping her," Jen said, lowering herself gingerly from the bed.

"Wait Jen, don't bother harass yourself too much. Remember you still weak," Mrs. Harmond warned.

"Is all right Mama, if ah just lie down an' look sick them not going to send me out of here so ah need to get out of this bed." She walked slowly and purposefully towards the nursery. She met the nurse coming back; her arms were empty.

"Where is the baby?" Jen asked slowly, uncertainly, a prickly moistness springing up in her palms and skin.

"The baby? Oh the baby," the nurse asked and laughed stupidly. "He is not inside there. I–I–I mean, he must be out here some-where." The nurse moved away and stopped at the first bed.

"Nurse!" Jen shouted, walking over to the nurse. "Ah just ask you for my baby! It look like you don't hear me good! Weh mi pickney deh?" She forgot the weakness and the tiredness and grabbed the nurse's sleeve.

"Let me go!" The nurse wrenched away her sleeve. As she moved there was a sharp sound as the sleeve was ripped down the front. The nurse looked at Jen angrily but her anger was not even a close cry to the look she saw glaring back at her.

By now everyone in the ward had been alerted by the voices and those standing, started moving towards the two like they were being pulled by an unseen magnet.

"Jen what happen? Where is the baby?" Mrs. Harmond pushed her way to the front and looked anxiously from Jen to the nurse.

"Mama she don't have the baby. She don't have the baby." She burst into tears and hugged her grandmother.

"What you mean she don't have the baby?" Mrs. Harmond asked, disbelief rising in her voice.

151

"Miss I'm going to check all the babies there must be a mistake somehow. Some mix-up take place. I will soon sort it out." The nurse moved away from the gathering and started going from bed to bed, checking each baby's hand-band and removing their diapers.

The sister on duty rushed into the ward. A nurse had rushed into the nursing station with the news of the altercation and the possible missing baby.

"What is the problem here?" she demanded, walking over to the nurse. Her voice held power and authority.

"When I went into the nursery I could not find the mother's baby." She beckoned to Jen. "There is no baby in the nursery so I am checking every baby out here."

"How many have you checked already?" the sister demanded, looking at the nurse.

"All of them on this side," she answered, indicating those on the left of the ward.

"Mother do you know your baby very well?" the sister asked Jen. "Is there any special mark or feature on the baby?"

"Yes nurse, she resemble me an' she have a mole right on the inside of her left hand and on her right foot bottom just like me and," she moved closer to the nurse, "she have a birthmark on her chest like her father."

Other nurses came to assist and soon they were quickly examining all the babies. The sister called two security guards and whispered something to them. They left in a hurry. While the search was going on in the ward, Jen flitted from bed to bed doing her own examination along with the nurses. The ward was as silent as an after interment scene except for the intermittent sniffling which came from Jen. Everyone watched nervously because if her baby was found it would mean that one of the other mothers had lost theirs.

One by one each mother was cleared. The nurses looked away from Jen and visibly jumped when Jen made a deafening scream that caused everyone's heart to stop suddenly, momentarily in shock. She fell to the floor and started kicking in a frantic manner like one in the throes of death. The nurses quickly grabbed her and one nurse left and came back with a needle in her hand. She gave her an injection and in a few seconds she became quiet and closed her eyes.

Mrs. Harmond and the girls watched as if from another place. They were attacked by numbness of the limbs and minds. The scene that had played out in front of them could not be happening to Jen, the family simply could not be hit with another loss.

Where could Jen's baby be? Who would want a baby from their cursed family? Or was it that the person wanted to kill the baby? Mrs. Harmond was expecting someone to appear with the baby and give a plausible explanation for her absence from the nursery.

The day ambled on and the hospital administrators closed off the hospital. No one could come in or go out except for medical personnel, patients and the police. They searched both sections of the hospital and the entire grounds, and searched everyone with a bag or anything that could conceal a baby. The search was unprofitable. The baby whom no one in the family but Jen had seen, had disappeared like a whiff of smoke.

Penalty For Crime

Mrs. Harmond sat in church and looked around her curiously. The service had not started as yet and there were little pockets of people locked in discussion. Mrs. Harmond did not join any of the groups, she knew what the subject was and was happy that at least she and her family were not the underlined topic. At least someone else was in the community's glare for a while. From where she was sitting she could clearly hear bits and pieces from different groups.

"You think him really going to come to church this morning?" It sounded more like a statement than a question.

"Boy I don't think so, him mus' really feel shame, really, really shame," the response came back.

"Well when other people meet dem waterloo him normally preach out about it and him don't expect people to stop from church when dem in the line of fire so him mus' come too." The first speaker was emphatic.

"But Jesus boy what a thing though! What a thing! All along some people believe that is only one family have rotten egg but look what happen! Jesus, the parson son!" The voice was incredulous, disbelief clearly rang out.

"You can imagine the boy do something like that! After him no hungry nor suffering like some of us. After him no barefoot or naked like some people. After him no live on road bank!" The anger in the speaker's voice rose to an agitated pitch.

Mrs. Harmond looked stealthily towards the voice and her mouth dropped open a little when she saw Cathy, Pete's girl-friend. She thought she had left the area since Pete's demise. She later learnt that she was still living at the house that Rita's sweat and blood had been shed to build, because she and her people were at war and they didn't want her back in her community. Mrs. Harmond looked away from her and shook her head slowly. She couldn't help feeling sorry for the now thin, gaunt woman.

The discussion and opinions were still raging. "Imagine the boy was tiefing all the time an' nobody never really know an' look how them catch him red handed an' carry him gone a prison!"

"Before him go to school him hide off down a river an' get himself mix-up with no-good, good for nothing wretches an' then when him leave school him have no qualification. You can imagine how parson embarrass although him should have really pay more attention to him own son instead of spending time in everybody business, him an' his two brother. Jesus ah hope nothing else no happen cause him mother sick so bad already." The voice was filled with concern.

The discussion confirmed what Mrs. Harmond had heard: the parson's son had been caught in a robbery in a supermarket in town. He was an employee at the supermarket and was the mastermind behind a series of removal of goods which had escalated

into a large scale robbery. Somebody had tipped off the proprietor
and he had laid a trap for him and his cronies.

There was a hush and all faces turned as if programmed by
a switch to the front of the church. It was the parson along with
his two brothers and the big man, Mr. Bently himself. They hardly
came to church and she wondered if they were there so that he
would not feel intimidated by his congregation. Well, Mrs. Harmond
thought they could certainly stop actual physical intimidation but they
certainly could not stop the silent questions and the disapproving
looks. Later, they could do nothing to boost the liveliness of the
service which sagged like a heavy burden imposed on slaves. The
singing sounded like a throng of tone deaf mourners wailing at a
funeral. The sermon, delivered by the parson himself, lacked the
burning evangelical fire which usually characterized the Sunday
services. Mrs. Harmond wondered why he had not asked one of
the other ministers to preach. He made neither direct nor indirect
reference to the matter as was his wont when anything untoward
happened in the community.

After the service everyone filed out. The parson's brothers
hurried him away without allowing him to walk around and shake
the hands of the people as he usually did. Mr. Bently did not leave
with them. He stood to one side at the gate glaring intimidatingly
at everyone. Mrs. Harmond walked as far from him as she possibly
could and ended up scraping her arm on the rusty, brown church
gate. While she was examining the abrasion, she looked up for a
while and met an arctic blast that chilled her heart. Why was this
man who had never spoken to her glowering at her as if she had
done him something personal?

*I wonder if he thinks my grandchildren are responsible for
corrupting the parson's son. Maybe I am too poor and ordinary*

looking or maybe because we are the scourge of the community,
the family that is cursed because it has done so much wrong that
nobody else in this world has ever done.

Instead of lowering her gaze she fixed him with what she thought was an equally frigid glare. She observed the look on his face; it was a kind of surprised shock. He had expected her to wilt and rush through the gate, but she took her time going through this time and even swivelled her head like a rotating fan and scowled at him anew. His face continued to be a study in surprise, but something new had been added, a questioning look.

Mrs. Harmond walked home with a myriad of thoughts plaguing her mind. She was toying with some ideas that had been floating around in her sub-conscious; they were becoming sentient thoughts and she planned to visit and mull over them when her mind was completely at rest.

When she got home, her grandchildren, except for Tyrone and Nickar, were gathered at her favourite spot under the tree discussing the latest community news. They seemed to be revelling in the fact that they were not the ones being slaughtered by the community. They were all animated except for Jen who was just a silent part of the group. She was just there looking on blankly with a vacant, lost look in her eyes.

Ever since her baby's disappearance, she had become a shadow, a mere form, stationary most of the time, floating around aimlessly the rest of the time. Mrs. Harmond was worried that she would become like Michanne. She was certain that the baby was alive somewhere and that one day they would find her and Jen would return to even a semblance of herself. The child's disappearance had forced Jen to reveal the father's name to the police, but when they had tracked him down he denied ever having a relationship with Jen and was aghast at the idea of him or anyone he knew abducting the baby. What would he want with a jacket which was not his, he asked the police. Mrs. Harmond did not join in the discussion. She knew better than to gloat at other people's misfortune. She knew that just like how her grandchildren had gathered to discuss the robbery and arrest, it was the same thing that other people did when they were on the receiving end.

The following morning, without knowing why, she woke up later than usual. She was annoyed with herself because she had planned to do some weeding in her yam garden that morning, and the earlier she started the better it would have been because the mid-day sun would come spitting its venom, which would reduce her to a dripping mass of frustration and drive her under the tree or indoors.

The house was unusually still. There were no sounds of the radio playing or the children talking or arguing. Mrs. Harmond peeped through the back door and saw them all gathered around Joan-Ann and Simone at the designated washing area which comprised of a huge wash basin placed on a massive tree trunk from a tree that had fallen in a hurricane. She wondered why they had all congregated at the spot and made to call to them but for some unknown reason, decided against it. She decided instead to steal upon them and see what they were doing.

They were so engrossed in whatever they were doing that they didn't hear when she came up behind them.

"What you all doing out here?" she asked quietly.

They swung around, fright and surprise etched on their faces. After the initial surprise they all formed a block as if keeping Mrs. Harmond from something.

"What really going on here? Can somebody really tell me? What you all stand up in front a me hiding?" Mrs. Harmond felt anxiety engulfing her. Needle points of pain started piercing her all over. She could not explain the sudden change in her feelings.

"Mama nothing don't happen, go back an' lie down," Jerome said, taking himself out of the human blockade and holding Mrs. Harmond's hand with the intention of leading her away.

Mrs. Harmond wrenched her hand from him and pushed him away. "What is going on in this place? What you all hiding in my yard?" She started pushing her way through the blockade and then she heard Tyrone's voice.

"Come Nick, come fast, come let we leave this place quick!"

Mrs. Harmond stopped in her tracks. "Is what happen? Why you leaving this place so quick? Is what happening here, some-body tell me quick!" She started pushing through again but stopped when she detected a movement towards the back of the blockade. She stopped pushing and walked around her grandchil-dren. Her mouth fell open when she saw Tyrone assisting Nickar away. He was holding him around the waist and Nickar was lean-ing heavily on him and limping.

"Jesus father! Nickar, Tyrone come back here! Is what wrong? What wrong Nickar, why you walking so?" Mrs. Harmond started after them with a half run and a half walk. Nickar turned around at the sound of the feet and Mrs. Harmond caught a glimpse of a peaky face with pain engrained in it. The eyes seemed to be only half opened and the hair look matted and hung in different directions.

"Mama come back here." Jen and Austin rushed after her, caught her and though she struggled with them, she could not loosen their grip.

"Let me go! Let me fine out what been happening in my own yard. What wrong with Nickar? Somebody was fighting here this morning, what happen?" She continued to wrestle unsuccessfully with her two grandchildren. During the struggle she looked down and then she exclaimed, "Blood! Jesus Christ blood! Is who cut Nickar? You better tell me or else ah going to lock all a you out of the house! You hear me!" This was a new Mrs. Harmond, serious and threatening.

"Calm down Mama, calm down and then we can talk," Jen begged.

"Talk! Talk! That's all I been begging all of you to do since ah come out a the house but you refuse to talk. So what you suddenly have to talk about? An' let go off my hand, the two boy gone already an' ah can't catch them again. Let go off my hand!"

They let go suddenly and she almost fell. They jumped forward and grabbed her again and when she had righted herself, she pulled herself free. She took a few steps towards the washing area and again Jen and Simone tried to block her.

"Lord Jen might as well we just tell Mama what we know cause it no mek no sense we hide it. It going to come out anyway," Jerome reasoned.

While he spoke Mrs. Harmond rushed around the girls and looked down at the wash basin. The gasp she made caused her grandchildren to close their eyes in embarrassment and fear. Her horror was such that she could hardly speak. When the words finally came they sounded like a drowning person spluttering water from his or her mouth. "You, you, you, were wash, wash, washing bloody clothes in my bath!" She hit out feebly at Joan-Ann who was standing close to her.

Joan-Ann shied away shame-facedly and looked away from her grandmother. The others huddled close to her, away from

161

their grandmother. Even Jerome was afraid to approach her in her fury.

Mrs. Harmond closed her eyes and tried to still the rush of her heart which was doing a frenzied movement like a boat caught in a storm and was being forced away from its mooring. This could not be happening, not again and not in this manner. Her silent fears had taken form, her subverted imaginings had taken shape, the frequent, unexplained abscences of Nickar and Tyrone which she had suspected were no good must have led to this. "Tell me something, why you washing bloody clothes in mi yard? Why you washing bloody clothes in this yard?" Her voice had ascended to an alarming pitch which was teetering on a scream.

Her grandchildren were shocked, they had never heard her like this before, the quiet harmony in Mrs. Harmond was fast ebbing out and no wonder, enough was enough.

Jen, like someone breaking a vow of silence, spoke up. "Mama, him and Tyrone come out a the bush just as we come outside this morning an' he was bleeding an' almost fainting an' Tyrone help him change him clothes an' then ask us to wash out the dirty one." She looked everywhere but at her grandmother.

"What, what happen to him why him bleeding? An' don't tell me no lie! Ah just can't stand a liar!" Mrs. Harmond pursed and unpursed her lips and looked accusingly at her grandchildren.

Jerome spoke up. "Well Mama, you know him don't really like me, but when ah ask him what give him that cut on him leg – there is a big, round hole in him leg – him say that he was standing by a place an' some men start shooting an' the shot catch him."

"Where that happen?" Mrs. Harmond enquired. "An' why him don't go to the hospital?"

"Them never say, as a matter of fact them never want us to ask them any question or really tell us anything, and they never really want you to find out anything either," Austin told his grandmother.

"You really think this is going to escape the ears and mouth of this community? Wait little bit and you will really hear the full story; just wait little bit. Ah tell you from that man that say him is their father put back him foot in this country I know that it spell trouble! Worse when him come round here an' then them start disappearing almost every day an' get facety when ah talk to them. Well if you can't hear in you ears, you must feel it in you skin! Just wait till we hear the rest a this story!" Mrs. Harmond looked from one to the other as if to make certain that her words had hit the mark.

Austin looked back at his grandmother as if she were a stranger. "Mama, you talking like you believe everything that people talk about us. You just believe everything bad bout Nickar and Tyrone. What if them telling the truth?"

"Austin look at me," his grandmother commanded. "Look at me an' tell me if you believe that Tyrone an' Nickar leave here every day to work honestly! You know as well as I do how them lazy. They don't want to fight their way through this life. They believe that things come easy an' they very well know that in this family nothing go like that. With our so-call curse we really have to go the extra mile. Stay there an' believe what you want but trust me it won't be long before we hear about what happen to him an' other people in this family. Mark my word, time clock is striking the hour, something must give someway somehow." With those words she went inside without a backward glance at them.

True to Mrs. Harmond's word, they soon found out what had happened but not in the way she expected. About an hour later she was sitting under the tree trying to work out certain things in her mind. She ignored the quarelling birds and tried to put some ideas she had together. Her thoughts were interrupted by a loud, piercing siren at the top of the hill. She wondered who was terribly sick or had died. All her grandchildren rushed out of the house into the yard and Austin and Jerome even started walking up the hill. They did not have to walk far and soon the siren stopped and they heard the sound of boots trampling their way down the hill. Austin and Alton rushed back down the hill and joined the others who were standing in the yard. Mrs. Harmond felt a prickling in her head and sweat from nowhere sprang up into her palms and all over her body as three police officers came into view. The dogs started to bark erratically but remained at the side of the house. They must have felt threatened by the revolvers the officers bore and the dour look on their faces. Austin nervously threw a stone at the dogs. It struck one on the foot and he yelped in pain and limped out of the yard, turning back every few steps to bare its teeth and yelp about the injustice shown to it.

The officers walked towards the family purposefully. When they got close to the group – all the children had retreated to their grandmother's side – they stopped.

"Good morning," the one at the front greeted them. Without waiting for a response or introducing himself he continued, "Is this the residence of one Nickar James and Tyrone James?"

Mrs. Harmond nodded, her tongue had somehow lost its ability to utter meaningful sounds. She watched the tall, sombre faced man whose face was filled with dents and scrapes of a lifetime, and whose eyes, like the power vested in him, had the ability to arrest and hold one against his or her will.

"What relation is Nickar and Tyrone to you?" the voice bellowed like a bull searching for a mate.

Mrs. Harmond mustered up courage and recalled her voice. "They are my grandsons."

"Where are they?" the officer bellowed again.

Mrs. Harmond was convinced that she would have hearing issues long after he had ceased speaking.

"I don't know," Mrs. Harmond answered truthfully.

"What you mean you don't know?" the officer fired back. "Our intelligence is that they came this way! You better talk fast or you going to prison for harbouring and aiding and abetting criminals!"

"Criminals, what they do? You barge into my yard demanding my grandsons but up till now you don't tell me what you want with them!" Mrs. Harmond stared boldly at the officer even though she could feel a slight tremor shaking her body.

Without answering her at once, he turned to the other officers. "Start searching the place. I will come in a while."

"You not searching my place without a warrant!" Mrs. Harmond jumped up and placed herself in front of the officers.

The spokesman pulled a piece of paper from his pocket and shook it in Mrs. Harmond's face. He then waved the officers forward. Jerome and the other boys followed at a safe distance. They had heard too many stories about incriminating items suddenly popping up out of nowhere.

"Ah still don't know why you are looking for the boys," Mrs. Harmond complained bitterly. "You come into my yard an' gone to search the place an' ah still don't know why."

The officer turned and looked at her accusingly, a tic starting at the corner of his mouth. "Your grandsons that you raise have been involved in robbery an' all kind of criminal activities with their no good father. We have been trying to catch them for some time now but them slippery like jello. Last night your good for nothing criminal grandsons and their demon father break into a house in town, residents just return from England. They start beating the man, but they did not know that his son, a licensed firearm holder, was in the house. He blazed the father first and the two boys run, but it is believed that one was shot. Intelligence says they came this way and this is their home so they must be around here somewhere. We are going to charge you for harbouring criminals any how we find out that they were here." His scornful glare almost made a hole in Mrs. Harmond, it was so intense and accustary.

"Charge me!" Mrs. Harmond was almost frothing with rage. "What you just tell me is the first time I hearing about it. When I am at my house I never know that I responsible for what young people out there doing!"

"Lock up mama for what?" Jen blurted out indignantly. "My grandmother is not a wrongdoer. If Tyrone and Nickar do anything wrong is not mama fault!" She gave him a dirty look.

"My grandmother is not a wrongdoer," Michanne added.

"Why don't you all shut your wretched mouth? I am going to arrest all of you if I find they were here, wretched virus on society!" He stomped off and started walking around the house, peering around every corner and examining the ground. Mrs. Harmond's heart dipped dramatically as he neared the washing area. She was in no way condoning her grandson's behaviour but she wished for her sake and the rest of the family that Jen had thrown away the bloody water and disposed of the clothes. The officer peered into the basin and as Mrs. Harmond watched, his face remained expressionless. She exhaled in relief but it was premature when she saw him stoop suddenly, bend over and peer closely at the earth. Her breath caught in her throat when he straightened up and shouted, "Officer Malcolm! Officer Gayle, come here right away!" His face looked excited and his nostrils were twitching fast.

"Yes Officer Parkinson?" The first officer ran up to him anxiously, looking around him as he did.

Without answering the officer pointed to the ground. The other officer who had come running joined them and together they examined the ground. It did not stop there, they followed what seemed like a trail past the back of the yard into her yam garden and beyond.

Mrs. Harmond and her grandchildren stood in a tight group without speaking or looking at one another. Fear had clamped their lips shut and was hammering harshly at their hearts. She did not know what they would find and how far they would go.

Officer Gayle came hurrying back. He was shouting into the phone, "Yes, yes, we are at the suspects' home and they were here. We are following a trail into bushes and we need more help." He gave the listener his location and then walked over to the family. "So you don't know anything about the young men eh! You don't know anything but there is blood eh! Wait till we are finished with you, harbouring criminals and pretending innocence!" He looked at them like one would look at a pile of sour garbage. He was a man filled with patriotic fervour and the conviction to stomp out wrong doing. Zeal burnt hotly in his black, wide eyes and his clean shaven face looked young and anxious. He did not leave them, but told them to sit. Mrs. Harmond surmised that he was afraid they would run away.

About half an hour later sirens again blared urgently on the road at the top of the hill. Again heavy boots trampled the grass

167

on the pathway to Mrs. Harmond's home. Again, about twenty officers, some sombre faced and intense, dressed in plain clothes and accompanied by ferocious hounds, followed the trail of blood into the bushes.

Without warning, the officer who was watching the family handcuffed Mrs. Harmond. Dumbstruck and with alarm in her eyes, she stared at the arresting officer. The adrenalin had stopped, her heart had stopped, and her breath seemed to have stopped, only the instant wail of her grandchildren filled the silence.

"What you doing with mama?" Jerome stepped forward and confronted the officer. "What you handcuff mama for? What she do? What she do?" The tears started down his face in a hot, meandering trail.

Michanne started wailing like a wounded animal caught in a trap. "You let go mama! Let her go! Tek that thing off her hand!" She picked up a stone and advanced towards the officer.

The others grabbed her and pulled her back muttering, "No Mich, no! Mich you mad, him will shoot you!"

The officer stood his ground and looked at the highly agitated girl. She seemed to be out of her mind, but he was not fazed. He looked at them all and he felt no compunction for handcuffing the old woman. Most of the times these old women were the ones who spoilt the grandchildren, being too permissive and refusing to correct them when they were doing wrong. For all he knew, she had hidden him somewhere but the dogs would certainly ferret him out.

Officer Parkinson came out of the bushes a little later and told the officer to take Mrs. Harmond to the station. His brusque command was greeted by fresh heart stopping wails which followed the officer and Mrs. Harmond up the hill.

Jerome ran back, took what money he had and what his grandmother had on her dresser, locked the house and then ran up the hill and caught them at the top because Mrs. Harmond was walking slowly.

It seemed as if the whole community for miles around had fringed the hill. Some were chattering loudly like the birds in Mrs. Harmond's tree and some just stood stupefied at the sight before them.

Who Dat, who was sitting at his vantage point in a tree shouted out, "Jesus, officer man where you going with Miss Harry after she a nuh bad woman!" He jumped down out of the tree and fell to the ground in his shock.

The officer looked at the outlandish attire of cut jeans pants, old, satin vest and sharp-pointed dressing shoes, and despite the seriousness of the situation, a smile stole over his face. He looked away from him and then back again. "If you don't shut you stupid mouth ah going to take you in as well," he threatened.

"You going to have to kill me dead first an' then carry me in but mi still a ask you what you a duh with poor Miss Harry hand them in a that iron cuff; after she a nuh criminal!" Who Dat refused to be silent.

Green Lizard too joined in the protest. "Oh God officer, Miss Harry don't trouble people. Is not her fault if her grandpickney dem bad. She is the only mother dem know, but she no grow dem to do bad. She is a church woman. Where you really going with the woman?" His surprise had got the better of him, not even the disapproving, no nonsense look on the officer's face could still his tongue.

Others joined in the protest. "Let go the old woman!"

"Why you don't go look for the real criminal?"

"Is dat this country gone to, young policeman a handcuff innocent old woman?"

The policeman became nervous at the unexpected outcry around him. He did not like the tone of the voices and the looks of disappointment, disgust and distress on the faces. He thought the people would have been on his side. He hurried Mrs. Harmond into the jeep amidst the increasing wails from her grandchildren and the deafening outcry from the crowd. He started the jeep nervously and then he held the steering tightly as the jeep began to wobble dangerously. He heard thuds and breaking glass. Somebody or some of the people were stoning the jeep. It was as though the idiots did not realize that he was not the only occupant of the vehicle. He fought to keep the vehicle under control and panicked when he looked outside and saw the sheer drop to Gully Deep awaiting him. Sweat dripped from his face and palms and he could feel his clothes becoming damp. He closed his eyes and stepped on the brakes. Miraculously it held.

He put his head on the steering wheel and closed his eyes. For the moment he was oblivious of the old lady sitting in the vehicle behind him. His only thought was that he had not been hurt. For a moment he thought he was gone. He soon remembered the lady at the back of the jeep and spun around as if he had been bitten by a bee. Despite his resentment, he would not like for her to get hurt on his watch.

"Are you alright?" he asked her timidly. She stared stonily at him without responding. The only signs of the trauma she had just been through were the tremulous hands and the huge, staring eyes that unnerved him and pinned him to the seat. He began to have second thoughts about her. How could anyone go through two such harrowing incidents and instead of remonstrating or berating him, just sit and look so defiantly, still bearing the iron shackles of imprisonment reminiscent of her slavery background.

He tugged his eyes away from her and turned to look through the back windshield. The rabble was still standing there. Unmoving from where he was, he could hear the faint hum of their voices. He was afraid of even opening the door, lest they attacked him. He did not want to go out there wielding his gun. He wanted to keep his training in mind. He took out his phone and called his boss.

"I am at the top of the road and there is a situation here. I am unable to move."

"Stay where you are and take evasive action if you have to," was the command. "Is the woman still in the jeep?"

"Yes, she is." He looked around at Mrs. Harmond anxiously.

"Keep her there. We will soon be out now. If you try to do anything rash, you might find yourself in trouble so keep a cool head." He hung up without waiting for a response.

As soon as he got off the phone he noticed that some people had surrounded the jeep. Growing angry, he wound down the window, reaching for his gun at the same time. It was all he had to prevent them from hurting him.

Seeing the gun the people pulled back but did not run away. They spoke from where they stood.

"Let go the lady or at least take the handcuff off her hand!" one man shouted, shaking his fist at the officer.

"Yes at least take the handcuff off. Suppose it was your innocent mother, would you want somebody to do this to her or your sister, daughter or woman? Even if you still going to take her to the station to question her, you don't have to treat her like prisoner. Release the woman, man!"

The officer looked at the angry, earnest face of the man and thought about what he had said. They did not really know if she had seen the boys even though the blood was at her house. Moreover, he continued to reason, if he took the handcuffs off she could not go anywhere, not when he had the gun. He looked around at the woman, he would have preferred someone more human, someone who would at least say something or protest a little. What was she trying to prove with those intense, probing eyes she was examining him with? Who did she think she was, some kind of Job type?

He reached over to her and she recoiled. He shrank back and looked at her, not certain how to proceed. She had rendered him nervous. He looked sideways at her. "All I want to do is to remove the handcuffs and make you feel more comfortable. I am not going to hurt you." He reached over to her and nervously unlocked the handcuffs. Mrs. Harmond's face was expressionless and she said nothing. She rubbed her hands vigourously.

Outside there was a loud cheer and cries of, "Let her outside so we can see her, is not she a the criminal."

He did not comply with that request, fearing they would somehow take her away and get him into more than one trouble. He just sat and looked at them. When they realised their wish was not to be granted, they became quiet and instead eyed him like a cat watching its prey.

A few minutes later, the people moved as if they had received a signal. Suddenly the crowd shifted from close to the vehicle and headed to the brink of the hill which led to Mrs. Harmond's house. They were pointing and talking excitedly.

It did not take long for the objects of their curiosity to come into sight. The police officer opened the door and stepped outside, seeming to have forgotten Mrs. Harmond. Mrs. Harmond sat where she was for a while and then she timidly opened the door and stepped down. The officer looked around at the sound of the door and went and stood beside her.

Mrs. Harmond looked at him with disdain and declared, "I am not going to run away, ah just want to see what is going on."

He looked away from her and this time he was the one who did not respond. There was no need to, she was not begging for a conversation, just stating a fact.

Mrs. Harmond watched the movement of the crowd and tried to catch bits of their conversation. Two words drifted across to her: 'catch him'. She leaned on the side of the jeep to prevent herself from crumbling to the ground. She wanted to go back into the jeep but shock and embarassment had curtailed her mobility. Even if she was being chased she could not move. So this was it, the epitomy of her suffering, the ignominious deed of her grandson, him being taken to prison in front of her and the whole community there to watch. There was nothing left, not even a vestige of dignity.

She watched as the crowd shifted from the brink of the hill and the first officers emerged with the dogs. Then came two officers carrying a human form between them. The crowd grew silent and moved to the sides of the road, allowing the officers free passage. They walked purposefully towards their parked vehicles which were only a short distance away from where the officer's jeep had ended up.

Mrs. Harmond watched as they advanced closer and closer, soon they were passing by her. She did not want to see but she was involuntarily drawn to the figure being slung between the two officers. His eyes were closed and his face looked almost pallid like a person whose life blood had drained out. His hair flashed to the rhythm of the officers' walk and there was blood all over his pants. Mrs. Harmond felt herself falling into an abyss. It got deeper and darker and then sucked her into the very bottom. She slumped to the ground, unconscious.

Some Truths Revealed

Laurine waved goodbye to her husband as he drove through the school gate. She watched the car until it disappeared and then she greeted the security guard at the gate and made her way to the classroom.

It was very early and none of the other teachers were there yet, so she sat down slowly and allowed her imagination to take off. First of all she thought about a name for the baby she was carrying. If it was a boy she would name him after his father and if it was a girl she would name her after her maternal grandmother. Her mother, Leila had laughed at the idea because Mrs. Harmond's Christian name, Ethline, was really old. Laurine defended her decision to her amused husband, stating that she loved her grandmother and that of all the women she had ever met she was the bravest and most honest, next to her mother of course. She contended that her grandmother was made of heroic mettle as only a heroine could have borne all she had and was still standing.

Her mind travelled back to the afternoon her mother had called crying that her mother had collapsed after being arrested and witnessing Nickar's lifeless looking body being slung by police officers. She recalled the weeks of hospitalization before her grandmother had regained what was left of her health. She could not forget the fight her mother had to go through to get her to stay with her for three months before allowing her to go back to Gully Deep. Nobody could understand why anyone would want to go back to that demented place with all the sad memories and the hardship of surviving from day to day. Her grandmother contended that she was not going to run away from anything and anyone, and that Gully Deep was the only home she had ever known and that she still had her grandchildren to see to.

Laurine grimaced at the thought of her grandmother's grandchildren, it was more like what was left of them. Shan was dead and so was Elton. Nickar was in prison and no one had seen or heard from Tyrone since the day he left with the wounded Nickar. Michanne, though greatly improved, had to rely on pills for mental and physical stability. Jen had become very quiet and withdrawn, speaking only to select people and Joan-Ann had gone to live with a young man, a past schoolmate, who claimed he was in love with her. She said he had been good to her so far. Jerome had finished his schooling and with help from her mother, was attending university. He came home as often as he could to see his grandmother; his dedication to her was commendable. Even though she and her brother were not as close to her as the other grandchildren, she still loved her and wished there was something she could do to ease the lifetime of burden which weighed her down like a dog with a heavy stone around its neck about to be taken to the river to be drowned. She made certain she gave her whatever she could at the end of the month and even bought a cellular phone for her so that she could call her at times. She vowed never to treat her mother like her aunts did, although Nickar's mother had visited for a week when Mrs. Harmond was in the hospital. Her mother, Leila, had really lambasted her for helping to destroy her mother's life by abandoning her children to her care. She had left in a huff claiming that her mother's fate had been decided by her father and husband, and not her.

Laurine heard a vehicle drive in and looked towards the parking lot. It was Miss Avery, one of the kindergarten teachers. The school was made up of two sections, the early childhood section and the primary school. She taught in the primary school while Miss Avery taught in the early childhood section. It was mornings like these when they both arrived long before anyone else that had started them talking and for over a year now they had become more than acquaintances, watching out for each other in the mornings and exchanging teaching ideas, discussing their students' abilities and escapades, and swapping community news. Miss Avery or Annette as Laurine now called her, had no problems discussing some of what happened in her wealthy family, but Laurine was very guarded about her family; not that she was ashamed but because she did not want to divulge their history and under-achievement in light of her colleague's shining family.

Although Annette was talkative about her illustrious family, Laurine had secretly formed the opinion that there was a hint of sadness about the girl, something about the family which she probably did not like. She decided not to pry but one morning she asked her why she bothered to work for a small salary when she could have easily worked in the family business and earned much more. Her answer had shocked her. She preferred to earn her own money which she was sure about and moreover it was a way of doing something worthwhile for her country. In addition, it was a getaway from her home, not that she did not love it, but it was a great opportunity to work with children whom she loved and also to get to meet ordinary people. She was not married because her parents disapproved of the one person she was interested in simply because he was not rich or had the right family back-ground. They had a more affluent, older person in mind whom she swore she would only marry if God himself was the officiating minister.

Laurine loved the little ones in Annette's class. There was one little girl in particular that she found alluring. She had an oval face with huge, round eyes that lit up in a twinkling, mischievous way. Her eyebrows and eyelashes were profuse and her still small baby mouth opened in a round wonder at the slightest thing. Laurine had never seen her father but she suspected that he must be of Indian extract as her dark, attractive mother did not resemble her in any way. She loved to draw and her little hands were always busy drawing barely discernable human beings and anything else that struck her fancy.

Laurine eased herself out of her chair and shouted across to Annette, "Hi Ann, I'm over here, I beat you this morning."

"Hi Mummy, you most certainly did. I don't know how you did it with that little girl growing so quickly inside you. I swear she has put on a pound since yesterday." She laughed and opened her classroom door. "I don't know how I managed to wake up so early myself." She pouted and shook her head, her shoulder length hair wagged in accordance to her mood like a dog wagging its tail.

Laurine looked at her and laughed. Even when she was pouting one could not fail to notice her beautiful, smooth face which was without blemish. "Why couldn't you sleep last night?" she said jokingly.

Annette's face became serious. "You ought to be glad you live in a quiet neighbourhood, because it is not that the neighbourhood is noisy but on our property it is perpetual daylight. There's always some business going on, vehicles going in and coming out and all kinds of other strange noises and people."

"Well, I thought that by now you would have got used to it," Laurine said with surprise.

"I try to shut out the activities but sometimes it gets extremely busy and you just cannot ignore the noises." She gave a heavy sigh like one tired of a situation. "One day I am going to launch out on my own and find some peace." Annette gave a little laugh.

"You, you are not going anywhere. You are too comfortable and more over you are too attached to your family, especially your mother." Laurine laughed playfully at her colleague and then sat down heavily on the extra chair at Annette's table.

At that moment a number of vehicles drove in. Laurine peeped outside and noticed that both vehicular and pedestrian traffic had picked up. Two parents came in with their children, greeted the teachers and left.

"Morning Auntie Ann," one little girl quipped. "Ah get new pencil," she announced, walking over and showing off her new pencil.

Annette hugged her. "Good morning Danica, what a lovely pencil! Who bought it for you?"

"My mummy," the little girl said proudly.

Another little girl came over and her huge eyes lit up with involuntary laughter.

"Morning Auntie, I get sweetie for you."

"Good morning Chaniek, you are very kind this morning. I am going to put up my sweetie for break, thank you," said Annette, giving her a hug.

Laurine looked at the little girl and her eyes lit up. She was such a delightful little girl with innocence shining out of her eyes. "Hi Chaniek," she said beaming at her. "How are you today?"

"Fine thank you," she replied, raising her eyes to Laurine. She walked away and started playing with the other little girl.

Laurine watched her, something from that child always reached out to her. She went off into a reverie but Annette soon brought her back to the present. They talked until the first bell rang and then they parted company.

Later that night Laurine marked some papers and went to bed. Her husband grumbled that she was not getting enough sleep and it was not good for the baby.

About half an hour after falling asleep she woke up and sat up suddenly. "My God," she said in a soft whisper. "My God."

Her husband who was a light sleeper also sat up with concern. "Are you alright? Is something wrong? Are you in pain?" He looked at her anxiously, worriedly.

"No Chad love, not yet." She sounded excited.

"So what are you so excited about?" He looked at her strangely.

"You would not believe it, I just know it. Listen to this." She whispered in his ears at length as if she were afraid to voice whatever had woke her up.

Chad exclaimed, "You don't really believe that! Can you prove it?" The excitement was contagious. He sat up fully and stared at her.

"I think so, I have an idea, something I will do tomorrow one way or the other."

The next morning, she called her grandmother and quite subtly extracted an important bit of information from her.

During recess she walked over to Annette's classroom and sat down. She had her snack with her and ate it while she talked to Annette. It was not the first time she was eating in Annette's classroom so Annette was not surprised at the visit.

"You have such a beautiful fist," she observed, looking at the chalkboard admiringly.

"It's not any prettier than yours," Annette joked back.

"How do you write in your register, cursive or script?" Laurine continued.

"I write both, you can see for yourself. I write cursive for the biographical information and script for the names." She handed her register to Laurine.

Laurine took it and opened the register, starting from the front she looked through unhurriedly, commenting all the while on the beautiful writing. She closed the register and further praised the neatness of the daily entries. The kindergarten principal called Annette to the office for a few minutes and while she was gone, Laurine walked over to where some of the children were eating and talked and laughed with them and helped them to clear their area before the bell rang.

That afternoon as soon as she got home, she called her mother and told her excitedly what she was sure she had discovered but was making certain about. She enlisted her mother's help and got it, hopeful that everything would get sorted out before she went on maternity leave.

Six weeks later, she arrived at school even earlier than usual. A little after she got there, three strangers in a Toyota Corolla turned up. They talked with the guard and sat in the vehicle and waited.

Laurine sat where she was in full view of the parking lot. She did not want to miss anything. Annette came next and because Laurine was not moving around unnecessarily, she came over and sat with her. She talked animatedly as she kept her eyes on the parking lot.

A number of teachers and parents started arriving after about ten minutes and then a black Honda SUV arrived and Chaniek's mother alighted followed by Chaniek. Before the driver, whom Laurine presumed was her husband could drive off, two of the strangers stepped out of the Toyota Corolla, walked over to him and held up something for him to read. He then climbed out of the SUV and walked in front of the men to the Corolla. The other strangers walked back to his wife and the child, and spoke to the lady and then they too walked over to the Corolla. The husband and the child were placed at the back between the strangers and his wife was placed at the front.

From where they were sitting, the two teachers watched the drama. Laurine knew very well what was happening but she pretended ignorance and showed the same surprise as Annette and everyone else who had witnessed the proceeding drama.

Annette was the first to speak. "Laurine I wonder what this is all about!" She sounded shocked to say the least.

"They have taken the whole family," Laurine said, trying to subdue the excitement in her voice.

"I am going to find out from the security what this is all about. You stay until I come back, don't harass yourself." Annette walked off briskly.

Laurine smiled to herself. She hoped everything would turn out right and she knew that as soon as she reached home her mother would come and give her the full details. She could hardly wait, it was going to be the longest day in history.

Annette soon came rushing back. "The security does not know much but he said they were plain clothes police officers. But he really does not know what they wanted with the family, that is anybody's guess."

And guess everyone did but they did not even get close to the truth. How could they? But Laurine did.

She called her mother before she left school to make sure she reached her house before she got there, but her mother was already there and so was her grandmother.

"Afternoon Mummy, afternoon Grandma," she greeted them eagerly. "I can't wait, please tell me everything quickly before I burst right open with anxiety!"

Her mother laughed and started the story. "Jen, mama and I were waiting at the police station when the police came in with the family. But before they came out another set of officers had come in with Mr. Hamilton."

"Who name Mr. Hamilton?" Laurine asked.

"The child's father, same wretch who said he had nothing to do with Jen or the baby's disappearance. They took him to another part of the station so that he couldn't see us." Leila shook her head and continued. "When the family came in and we saw the little girl, Jen and mama jumped up right away and started to walk towards her. But the officers told them to sit and they went and stood by Jen and mama, and warned them to behave themselves."

"I can understand how they must feel, especially Jen," Laurine's husband said.

"Ah tell you something else," Leila continued. "Except for the brown eyes and the long lashes, the little girl is the carbon copy of Jen."

183

"Is the same way Jen was pretty when she was little," Mrs. Harmond said. "Same way. Even the police dem say afterwards that the little girl kill the mother dead stamp."

"So what did the police really say to the family at the beginning?" Laurine asked, not wanting to miss any bit of the drama.

"They asked both parents if the child was theirs and they both said yes. Then they asked them her date of birth and where she was born. They gave the same date of birth that you saw in the register, but said that the child was born at the university hospital. I suppose that the downtown maternity hospital too cheap for them." Leila's tone showed what she thought of misplaced pride. "At that point the officer warned them to tell the truth and life would be easier for them. One officer asked them where they had got the baby and the mother started crying. She said she had done nothing wrong. The police told her about the DNA testing which had been done and they wanted to know how this was possible without their knowledge. They further told them that the DNA showed that the child was Jen's daughter which had been stolen from the hospital. They also asked them to look at the child and look at Jen. At this point the mother was crying uncontrollably. A female officer told her about the birthmark and took the child and the lady away to verify this. It was there as plain as the earth we walk on."

Leila paused for breath and Mrs. Harmond said, "Ah really feel sorry for the lady though cause she was not the one that steal the child."

Laurine looked at her grandmother and shook her head, thinking at the same time, my grandmother is always thinking about other people even when they do not care for her.

Leila continued. "Well after the questioning it turned out that the lady can't have any children of her own so when her cousin,

Mr. Hamilton, who was already married with a family, brought the baby to them and told them that the mother, a dear friend of his, had died giving birth, and that she hadn't known who the father was and since there was no family, they could keep the baby. He even went as far as helping them to adopt the child."

"That's why I said ah was sorry for her." Mrs. Harmond's pity for the lady was evident.

"Yes, she was crushed and as a woman my heart goes out to her, but think of Jen and our family and what we have gone through. As soon as they have gone through the legal ranglings, Jen will get back her child. In the meantime the child will stay with me and Jen can visit her as much as she wants to. Because of your involvement Laurine, it was suggested that she goes to another school." Leila leaned back in the chair having told all.

Laurine looked from her mother to her grandmother. It was the first in a long time that she had seen a genuine smile on their faces. She felt especially happy for her grandmother. She wondered if with a new generation fate would consider smiling in the family's direction.

The Graves Give Up Their Dead

Mrs. Harmond woke up suddenly and for a while she was disoriented. As her eyes settled on her surroundings, she realized that she was in bed. She had just had one of the recurring dreams. In this one, some black bats had been closed up in a building for years. They kept flying in every direction trying to free themselves but could not. It was very pathetic to see their frenzied movements and hear their melancholy cries. Then without warning, a bat from outside flew in and the other bats found the hole, and with a fearful screeching they all flew out. As soon as each one reached outside it became a dove which winged its way to further freedom.

The other recurring dream was of a family in a house by the seaside. The house was in a quagmire and started sinking. The family jumped into a boat which carried them away from the sinking house. They rowed to safety and watched as the house disappeared into the ground.

Mrs. Harmond looked at the time, it was only after midnight. She found it difficult to sleep and lay listening to the night noises. An owl hooted repeatedly and gave the night an eerie feeling. Some insects, led by the crickets, chorused incessantly like people at a wake who had no intention of going home until daylight. Clearly there were visiting dogs who were involved in a dispute, their barks were sharp, insistent, intentional statements of discontent. They doused the sounds of the other creatures and soon their snarls signalled the start of a savage fight. Mrs. Harmond got out of bed, opened the window and shouted at them but to no avail. She took up on old shoe which she hardly wore and threw it at them. There was a short, sharp yelp and then the barking lessened but in a few minutes it started up again, further away from the house.

Mrs. Harmond, now fully awake, started to do some hard thinking. For some time now she had started putting some ideas together based on observation and a few things she had learnt. When she had gone to the hospital, her bed had been next to a woman who worked at the house of one of the most affluent persons in the parish. By pretending to sleep, she had overheard a half whispered conversation about some strange activities in the parish. At first some of it did not make sense to her but as time went by some things began to take shape in her mind and she was certain of some answers but had no proof. Also fear held her captive; how could she a member of the plebeian class move against the mighty ones? Dread and indecision ruled her being but she argued with herself and decided to act.

She suddenly realized that there were no sounds from the birds. She rose and looked up into the tree and then walked around it and stretched her neck to giraffe proportions to see if they were sitting silently for some reason, but there were no signs of even one bird. She considered calling Simone but thought better of it.

She sat down again, took out her phone and started dialling a number but stopped halfway through when the dogs started barking and running up the hill.

"Michanne! Simone!" she shouted loudly. "Come out here now, ah think the dogs gone after somebody!" She got up and looked towards the top of the hill and made out two forms. "Michanne! Simone! Come right now!"

The girls came running and started up the hill, calling to the dogs at the same time. The dogs came running back and the girls stood where they were. The two forms stopped by them and then they came towards Mrs. Harmond who was still standing in the yard.

Mrs. Harmond stared at her visitors. In all her days she had never seen Miss Monica and her daughter at Gully Deep. Miss Monica was the person who took care of the parson's mother and as a result, thought of herself as part of the middle class. She didn't look very proud at the moment and Mrs. Harmond noticed that her eyes were red and that tears lurked in the corners. Right away she knew that the parson's mother had died, but what she could not understand was why Miss Monica had come to her home.

"Sister Harry," she began and then the sniffling started.

"What happen Miss Monica? What happen?" Mrs. Harmond wanted confirmation.

"Lawd Sister Harry, Sister Lurline dead! Sister Lurline gone!" She started sobbing loudly, the tears racing from her eyes in a great rush.

"Oh Jesus, ah really sorry to hear, ah really sorry. But look at it this way, she been suffering for years and could barely even talk, so the dear Lord give her rest and peace!"

"That is really true Sister Harry, really true but she was like mi mother an' ah miss her for true."

Mrs. Harmond allowed her to vent her emotion and then she asked softly, not wanting to rush her, "What really bring you here, you just passing or what?"

Miss Monica sniffled some more and then she beckoned to Mrs. Harmond to move away from everyone who had gathered to listen.

Mrs. Harmond followed her, her eyes a round question mark. She did not understand what was happening.

Miss Monica cleared up the mystery. "Before she died, an' you know she could hardly talk, she call me an' whisper slowly in my ears. Ah write down what she say an' she said ah shouldn't tell you anything till she dead." She handed a folded piece of paper to Mrs. Harmond.

Mrs. Harmond took the paper and clenched it in her palm. She would read it when Miss Monica left, not before.

Her task done, Miss Monica left. Mrs. Harmond still held the clenched paper and she had a very good idea what it said but decided to read it when she was alone. She asked her grandchildren to do something on the inside and then sat down under the uncannily silent tree. She stared at her clenched fist and then she opened her palm. The piece of paper was crumpled and slightly wet from her sweating palm. Nervous, excited and apprehensive, she unfolded the note and held it close to her eyes as if she were short sighted. The writing was atrocious but she could read the hasty scrawl. *Sister Harry, if you check G land you will find a part of the answer. The other part, the female one, is a part of me.*

Mrs. Harmond sat stupefied for a few minutes and then she sprang up like a tall figure which had been squashed into a very small container and had been suddenly released. She almost walked fast as she went into her room. She called her daughter and then she started packing a bag. She got ready quickly and then went and sat under the tree.

"Ah have to go up to Leila to look bout some urgent business," she said evasively.

"All of a sudden so Mama!" Simone asked, looking at her queerly.

"Well the time has come for me to act. The time has really come." She did not look at Simone.

"Act doing what Mama?" She looked at her as if she had gone mad.

"Ah really can't explain but you will soon understand."

Simone shrugged her shoulders and walked into the house. Soon Leila arrived and Mrs. Harmond went away with her. She told her to stop by Laurine's house because she wanted her to be a part of the plan. When they got there they went to sit in the backyard because they did not want to wake up Chaniek and the baby. Jen was staying with Laurine for the time being and had found a job in town. The social worker had insisted that she had to get a job and better living conditions or else they would keep the baby. Laurine allowed them to stay with her.

Mrs. Harmond showed them the note and they started the discussion.

"But Mama why she never just come out and say exactly what she mean?" Leila asked, looking perplexed.

"No Leila, she couldn't do that, cause Miss Monica would know too much," Mrs. Harmond answered.

"Exactly," said Laurine. "I think she know you could figure it out, but Miss Monica don't know what she was talking about so she can't broadcast it."

"Mama, do you know what or where is G land?" Leila asked.

"Yes ah know, an' ah had a queer feeling about the place a long time ago cause of something in the past but later for that." Mrs. Harmond had a distant, sad look in her eyes.

"But Mama what about the second part. That is a little bit confusing." Laurine screwed up her face and looked at Mrs. Harmond with expectancy.

"That one ah did kind of guess when Shan dead. Ah always know that that person know something. Talk a little bit too much," Mrs. Harmond said slowly, sadly. "Don't know how my dear sister find out but it haunt her to her grave just like how it bother me cause ah never had any proof, neither could I touch him."

"But who is that Mama? You need to tell us, this suspense going to kill us." Leila could not contain herself. She got up and walked around agitatedly.

Mrs. Harmond wrote on the note and handed it to Laurine. She took it, scrutinized it and then gasped. Leila rushed over and did the same thing.

Before they could speak Mrs. Harmond said two things. "Leila, you need to get your husband police inspector friend to talk to me." She paused and looked at her daughter and granddaughter's disbelieving faces. "Laurine you need to get your teacher friend to go away from G land cause she sound like a nice girl an' ah don't want her to get caught up in this attaclapse."

"Jesus Father." Laurine was astounded. She stared at her grandmother as if she had just fallen to earth from a UFO.

E E E

The crowd pressed forward like a wave in a storm surge. They pressed excitedly against the yellow rope which defined their limit and confined them yards away from the digging. The asperity of the police officers kept them from crowding around the grave diggers who were not digging graves for anyone to be interred, but were digging up bodies.

Mrs. Harmond and the members of her family were not standing with the crowd, they were standing in the privileged position beside the police officers who were close to the diggers. After a few feet down the diggers let out a shout. The shovel had connected with something. The digging became more frenzied and so did the movement of the crowd. The diggers gave a shout again and backed away suddenly, and the crowd let out a piercing scream.

"Take them out! Take them out!"

"Free them, them down there too long!"

The diggers went forward again and this time they came up with different parts of a skeleton. Some of the police officers backed away but Mrs. Harmond stood her ground. The tears which had been trapped in their iron container were at last released. They gushed like flood water in spate, unheeding, unchecked, hot and healing. Through her tears she looked at Mr. Bently and the parson's two brothers who were looking on, seemingly unabashed. They were handcuffed and stood between two police officers. Mrs. Harmond chided herself for not feeling sorry for them, especially Mr. Bently who had long ago started the siege on her family, robbing her of a father, a husband, a son and a grandson. He had confessed to his crimes and Mrs. Harmond knew that her husband and son had died innocently. Mr. Bently, even in his old age, still headed the drug syndicate he and the parson's father had started in their youthful days. Her father used to do odd jobs for him on the weekends and had stumbled upon some incriminating evidence. He and three others had been lured to sea, murdered and then taken back to Mr. Gustus' property and buried. Her husband had somehow found out about his father-in-law's death and had suffered a similar fate. Markdon had gone to town sometime after Shanae's death and while using the public bathroom had overheard some men talking about the parson's older brother who had been involved with Shanae and then had her taken care of because she had become pregnant and was threatening his marriage. The men had seen him coming from the bathroom. One of them was an affiliate of the parson's brother so Markdon had been trailed and killed, and laid to rest in the same burial ground as his father. Elton had sinned when he refused to give over his ganja to Bently's men for a cheaper price, instead of buyers of his own choice.

Mrs. Harmond was roused from her ruminating by another shout. The crowd kept surging forward and the yellow line broke but the police drove them back. One by one the diggers unearthed the skeletons. Later, if it were possible, they would be identified. In all they had unearthed six skulls.

$$E \ E \ E$$

It had been a hot day. Nature had lent its light to uncover the dark deeds of the past, but dissatisfied at what had been revealed, it scowled threateningly, angry at the evil deeds of mankind. As soon as Mrs. Harmond and her family started down the hill to her house, the rain started in partnership with the lightning and thunder which shouted their outrage in no uncertain manner.

The family started to run, Jerome held Mrs. Harmond's hand and she tried to move quickly. As they approached her favourite tree, a peal of lightning like a barrage from an automatic weapon, struck. There was a splintering, crackling sound as the tree split in two and started to burn. Everyone started to scream and ran towards the house but it would offer them no shelter, it too was on fire.

They ran back screaming and made for the butchery. They crammed inside as the rain stopped. They watched in utter shock as the fire roared through the house in vengeance, consuming the whole structure and everything within.

A New Beginning

t was the belief of many that fire cleansed and forced people to make a new beginning; to pick up themselves and whatever they could salvage from the ashes and build again. It helped people to rethink their lives and the mistakes they had made so that they could live again, but not with the thought that there would be perpetual happiness, because that precious commodity only came in small pieces, not huge chunks like sadness.

Mrs. Harmond sat on the verandah of her new house looking at the sunset. The clouds were all out in their coloured glory: purple, orange, yellow and indigo. They kept the dark of the approaching evening at bay and allowed the sun to glow gently in its fading yellow orb.

Mrs. Harmond turned around and looked at the house. It was built on a lot, next to her daughter Leila, by the government and individuals sympathetic to their suffering. It was a comfortable four-bedroom with two modern bathrooms, living and dining rooms, a spacious kitchen and washroom.

Her eyes filled with tears as she listened to the happy sound of Chaniek playing with Laurine's baby, whom she looked after during the day. Jerome was home and was playing soft, inspirational music as he studied. Jen and Simone had gone to work in the beauty parlour they had started in town. Michanne was a trainee in the food and beverage field, and Melvin and Austin were involved in construction.

Mrs. Harmond felt her years pressing her down but smiled with satisfaction because like Job, she had risen from the rubble of loss and misfortune, still holding on to hope and faith.

GLOSSARY

Abner: A baby ghost.

Butchery: A small outhouse used for storing ground provision, farm equipment etc.

Wanga gut: A greedy person who goes around eating from just about anybody.

Planting: Carrying out rituals to ensure that a ghost does not go around giving trouble.

Attaclapse: Big trouble.

John crow baking
bread to eat him: A very meagre person; somebody who looks very much like skeletal remains.